CALIFORNIA PASSAGE

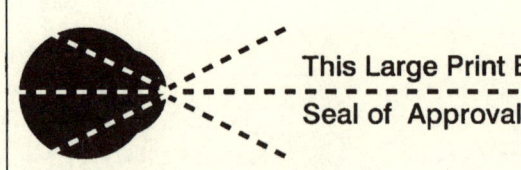

This Large Print Book carries the Seal of Approval of N.A.V.H.

CALIFORNIA PASSAGE

CLIFF FARRELL

Thorndike Press • Waterville, Maine

Copyright ©, 1957, by Cliff Farrell
Copyright ©, 1957, by Curtis Publishing Company
Copyright © renewed 1985 by Mildred Farrell

A serial version of this story appeared in
The Saturday Evening Post

All rights reserved.

Published in 2002 by arrangement with
Golden West Literary Agency.

Thorndike Press Large Print Paperback Series.

The tree indicium is a trademark of Thorndike Press.

The text of this Large Print edition is unabridged.
Other aspects of the book may vary from the original edition.

Set in 16 pt. Plantin by Elena Picard.

Printed in the United States on permanent paper.

Library of Congress Cataloging-in-Publication Data

Farrell, Cliff.
   California passage / by Cliff Farrell.
     p. cm.
   ISBN 0-7862-4885-8 (lg. print : sc : alk. paper)
   1. Wagon trains — Fiction. 2. Trappers — Fiction.
3. Large type books. I. Title.
PS3556.A766 C35 2002
813'.54—dc21   2002035864

CALIFORNIA PASSAGE

Chapter I

Ellen Jessup fought terror and panic. Standing in the dimness of the crude lodging she had rented at the establishment known as the Overland Inn, she peered through a tiny slit in the frayed length of oiled paper which served as a window shade.

From this concealment she had a view down upon the principal street of Independence. Early dusk had come and the respite from the blazing heat of the August day had stirred the amazing activity below into new, feverish life.

Vehicles of all varieties, from great, ox-drawn prairie wagons to varnished phaetons, inched along hub-to-hub, with the drivers in short-tempered competition. Wheels churned and rechurned the powdery dust. A steady current of humanity on foot flowed and eddied along the narrow duckboard and clay sidewalks.

She watched a man emerge from the

street door of the inn almost below her window and go strolling along with the throng. A moment earlier she had heard this same person leave a room not far from her own, lock the door, then pass along the hall and down the inner stairs on his way to the sidewalk.

She drew back a little, fearing that the very intensity of her gaze might warn him of her presence. But he moved off down the street without a glance upward. He was a stockily built man with graying hair and heavy, impassive features. Every item in his garb — stout store suit, dark felt hat, soft white shirt, snap-on bow tie and heavy-soled shoes — was scrupulously commonplace. He could have been a storekeeper or a salesman — but Ellen knew now that he was neither.

She was now certain that she had been followed all those miles from Baltimore and that her every move was being watched. She had noticed that same man during the furtive, roundabout journey she had made by train and stage to Pittsburgh. She had glimpsed him again on the levee at Cincinnati during the overnight stop.

She had hoped that it was only coincidence, but fear had remained with her during the remainder of the journey. Now he was here in Independence, occupying a room at the inn only a few doors from her own. No, there was no longer any doubt.

Now that she had something tangible with which to come to grips she calmed and the panic ended. She had lived with phantoms for so long that this actual imminence of danger was almost a stimulus to her.

She tried to visualize what the graying man's next step might be — and estimated her own ability at counteracting it. Excitement stirred warmingly in her. Color moved up from her throat and eased the taut set of her straight mouth, softening her lips. Becoming aware of this new emotion, she was almost appalled. "Am I actually enjoying this awful thing?" she asked herself accusingly.

She had been so carefully taught to be always lady-like, to avoid scenes and to swoon at the mere thought of violence. She was shocked by this discovery of a lawless strength within her.

She returned to the viewpoint at the window. The figure of the stranger had disappeared.

She had drawn her thick, dark hair into a rigid bun at the back, and had thinned and arched her brows and added shadow beneath her eyes and used rouge and rice powder on her lips and cheeks. All this helped dull the clarity of her dark eyes, added age to her appearance and blurred the sensitive slenderness of her features.

She wore cheap earrings and a gaudy bracelet. The wedding band on her third finger was already tarnishing. She had purchased them in the same backstreet racket store in Cincinnati where she had bought her wardrobe. The indifferent fit of the rather flashy skirt and the off-color cotton blouse could not entirely hide the fact that she was straight-limbed and attractively contoured.

There was the mark of deep-rooted finishing school training in the way she carried herself. Back in Baltimore she had been considered quite a beauty.

Her attention was caught now by another man who was moving along the opposite sidewalk. She had noticed this person earlier in the day and there were reasons why she had become interested in him, reasons that had to do with her own plans and her own safety.

She had first seen him enter Independence that morning, riding a wild, tough-mouthed sorrel horse that was fitted with a Spanish saddle. He was leading four heavily laden pack ponies. To her Eastern eyes he presented a wild and bizarre spectacle. His own blue eyes had been arrogant and challenging as he rode down the street. It was as though he scorned this place and considered its inhabitants his inferiors.

A ragged elkskin hunting shirt hung from his lean, wide shoulders. He wore buckskin breeches that had been shrunken by time and weather until inches of his bare shanks were exposed above his moccasins. He was unshaven, and his tawny hair was bleached the color of straw by exposure. His skin was tanned a contrasting hue of deep bronze. He was whip-thin.

Obviously, he and his ponies were completing a long and harsh journey. And it was also obvious that this was not the first time of such hardships for him.

Ellen then lost track of him for a few hours. When she noticed him again, his appearance had changed amazingly. He evidently had visited a barber and found a bathtub in the meantime. His long jaws were scraped smooth, and his hair was trimmed short so that his ears were very prominent. He had an aggressive chin and a nose and mouth to match. His forehead was high, his brows straight.

He was taller than most men, and Ellen decided she had never seen a person who seemed to move so indolently and yet with such easy grace. Nor one so gaudy in his raiment. He now wore a beaded hunting shirt that had been stretched almost to the thinness of woven cloth, tanned to the softness of velvet and dyed a rich cream color. It bore open lacings of white elkskin thongs at the sides for coolness. Below that he wore dark blue Mexican charro breeches of a fine linen weave, also with white laces in the wide slashes in the bell bottoms. Around his waist was knotted a red sash of fine, thin, fringed silk. The boasting display of the trophy of some amorous conquest during his wanderings, Ellen decided. In the sash was thrust a very practical cap-and-ball pistol and a bone-handled knife. He wore gaudy moccasins with high, rolled tops of white fawnskin. Ellen had discreetly inquired about him at a mercantile where she had shopped during the afternoon.

"Oh, him!" the storeman had sniffed. "That's one of them trappers. Name is Luke Storm. Shows up here sometimes to sell his plews an' dance an' drink an' sing. Risks his hair in the mountains for months at a stretch, then blows in all the profits in two, three days."

"A man like that," Ellen had said musingly, "might know all the trails to California and the quickest way to get there."

"He ought to," the storeman had said. "He sure ought to."

Luke Storm was a person who could not be overlooked easily, even in this crowded town. And he seemed to be taking pains to make sure he would be noticed. All afternoon he had been making the rounds of the inns and fandango houses and monte banks. He was flushed now with drink, but seemed as steady as ever on his feet as he moved boisterously along.

He jostled men aside who did not veer out of his path and dared them, with a hopeful glint in his eye, to take offense. He ogled any comely females who came in sight. This drove the majority of them into taking cover in shop doorways, or to hurrying, with averted eyes, to the opposite side of the street. Even so, Ellen noticed with disapproval, many half-wistful and furtive glances followed him from beneath bonnet brims.

She became nettled when a bare-shouldered dancehall girl emerged from a doorway, attached herself to Luke Storm's arm and attempted to cajole him inside. He swung her high with a whoop and sent her on her way with a resounding spank.

The thought occurred to Ellen that it would be quite a pleasure to slap the face of this conceited barbarian and put him in his place. He was so blatantly sure of his physical prowess.

He had already been in trouble a couple of times. Early in the afternoon she had seen a swirl of excitement at the door of a monte house. Luke Storm had appeared, bearing aloft the struggling weight of a tinhorn gambler whom he hurled into a horse trough. Later on he had been the center of what evidently had been a general, free-for-all brawl in a tavern. And he still seemed to be inviting trouble.

Ellen's gaze became smokily critical. Luke Storm's manner offended all her sense of decorum. He was apparently a very overbearing person who represented every trait that she had been taught to abhor. He was thoroughly detestable — and yet she must ask of him a great favor.

She now heard faint, shuffling movement in the bare-boarded hall outside her door. Her first thought was that it might be the stocky, gray-haired man. She lifted her reticule from the bureau, opened it and let her hand rest against the cool assurance of a short-barreled pistol inside.

Directly beneath her room was the tavern where men were drinking and gambling. The tumult of their voices and activity came in a steady rumble — a sound that had never ceased, day or night, during the three days she had occupied these quarters.

Though she used an outer stairway at the rear of the two-story building in coming and going to her room, she had learned to keep her door bolted. There had been occasions when other footsteps had halted outside and hands had tested the knob, seeking entrance.

She waited, feeling tension slide its coils, one by one, around her. Then a hand tapped timidly.

"Who is it?" she demanded guardedly.

A small, gulping voice responded. "It's me, missy! Tansy White."

Ellen drew a long, sighing breath. Her knees were shaking. She drew the bolt and cautiously opened the door an inch. She dropped the pistol out of sight in her reticule and admitted a tiny, barefooted Negro lad of about twelve.

Tansy White was chore boy at the tavern. He was almost in tears. He thrust a small envelope into her hand. "I's too scairt, missy!" he blubbered. "Dat man'd eat a boy like me alive. I jus' couldn't do it." He tried to hand her a sweaty small coin.

Ellen had to smile. "You keep the money, Tansy," she said. "And here's a quarter also, just for you. But there was really nothing to be afraid of. He'd have had me to deal with if he tried to frighten you. You run along home now. It will soon be dark."

She added, as the lad scuttled for the door, "And Tansy, I'd be sad if you said anything about this to anyone. This will be just our own little secret. Promise?"

Tansy promised and fled gladly.

After the door closed, Ellen stood for a time in indecision. Then she determinedly pinned on the daisy-trimmed straw bonnet and the candy-stick jacket that were a part of her new wardrobe. She looked at herself in the small mirror. Her heart failed a little as she remembered the fine linens and the cool, flimsy dresses of lawn and lace, the elegance of watered silk, she had known in the past.

She picked up her reticule. She hesitated, then moved to the small trunk that held her few belongings. Delving into it, she brought out a dirk with a five-inch blade cased in a small leather and velvet sheath which was equipped with clips so that it could be attached to a lady's garter.

She had bought both pistol and dirk at Cincinnati. The pistol was of a new type that used five metal-bound cartridges instead of the cumbersome cap-and-ball method of loading. The proprietor of the gun store had assured her that this weapon would stop most any human being. But when she had insisted on buying the dirk also, the man had edged away from her a trifle. Evidently, in his opinion, it was perfectly proper for a lady to carry a pistol with which to shoot annoyers in the stomach. But there was a line of demarcation. Women who had knives slung from their garters were not regarded as respectable.

Ellen flushed a little at the recollection. Then she lifted her skirt and fastened the sheathed dirk securely above her knee. Its weight was a comfort.

Carrying her reticule on her arm, she listened at the door until sure the way was clear. Then she left the room, hurried down the hall and descended the rear outside stairway which overhung an ash-heap alley. This brought her to a narrow walkway, between the walls of the tavern and an adjoining harness store, which led to the street.

It was the hour between deep twilight and full darkness. Window lights blazed, and the dust spume was a golden network in these yellow bands. The wheeled traffic was diminishing, but the restless flow of foot movement was increasing. The gambling houses were beginning to roar.

Ellen moved along the street in the direction she had seen Luke Storm heading. She carried in the bosom of her waist the message which Tansy White had failed to deliver. Now she meant to deliver it herself.

Suddenly she came face-to-face on the crowded sidewalk with the gray-haired man. He was returning toward the Overland Inn, strolling along, a pipe in his mouth. Except for the briefest flicker of what may have been dismay, his glance passed casually over her and he continued on his way. But she sensed that he had not expected or wanted this close meeting, and that his mind was instantly pondering her purpose in appearing at this hour alone among this rough company.

Her own pulse was pounding, and she had to call upon all her resolution to avoid hurrying. Presently she risked a glance back. There was no sign of him. She continued ahead. When a freight wagon intervened, she used it as a shield in darting to the opposite sidewalk and then down a dark side lane.

This street was nearly deserted. A blacksmith shop was still open, and in its depths she saw two sooty men intently occupied in sweating a tire on the wheel of a Conestoga wagon. Their forge fire spilled a rusty illumination through the open shed doors.

Ellen took refuge in the lee of one of those outflung doors and found a crevice through which she could peer. Soon she saw the square silhouette of the gray-haired man pass by on the main street. As she had anticipated, he had retraced his steps in an attempt to follow her. He was stretching his neck, scanning the sidewalks ahead.

After a few minutes she saw him again, returning toward the center of town. He was now walking fast, with the air of a worried man.

She had eluded him for the time at least. She returned to the street. She now saw that she was near the outskirts of town. Wagons, singly and in groups, were camped on the open flats beyond the last scatter of buildings.

One organized company of some thirty canvas-hooded prairie schooners was drawn up in horseshoe formation. Campfires blazed brightly here. Ellen heard the deep voice of a man intoning a prayer. Then came the clear lift of a girl's voice, singing a hymn. She was accompanied by the throbbing strains of a harp.

A general drift of movement was setting in toward this camp, for this wagon company was scheduled to set out at dawn for faraway California. In spite of the lateness of the season, these stampeders were gambling that they could make it through to the gold fields before the mountains snowed in. And Ellen intended to accompany them.

Then she sighted Luke Storm's lank figure ahead, moving in the same direction. She hurried eagerly to overtake him.

Chapter II

Luke Storm was unaware that such a girl as Ellen Jessup existed.

He had come in that morning from a thousand miles of steady travel, leading his pack string laden with pelts and trapsacks. He had sold the whole kit and caboodle to a trader for six hundred dollars, with a jug of fine New Orleans rum and a pound of honeydew smoking tobacco to boot.

The rum was gone, the jug smashed. And the biggest part of the money had been gambled over the monte tables or thrown to the girls in the fandango houses to see them scramble.

He had never been a provident man, for the life he had led had taught him to enjoy each moment to its utmost and to let tomorrow bring its own promises. For, in his profession, tomorrow was a day that might never come. He had seen so many of his kind go. An arrow from a coulee, the terror of a war whoop at dawn, a loosened avalanche on some bleak mountainside . . . starvation . . . thirst . . .

He was driven now by an even greater recklessness. He was a man who, at the age of twenty-eight, found himself at the frayed end of nowhere. The old days were gone and even he stubbornly had to admit it. Beaver plews were hardly worth the cost of the wear and tear on the traps that caught the creatures. Men now wore silk hats and females adorned themselves in bundles of silk and satin and crowned their bonnets with the feathers of birds from unknown tropical lands. When the ladies wanted furs it had to be seal or sea otter, and the Russians had that trade sacked up.

There was no longer money in hunting or trapping. There was no place, apparently, for a man like Luke Storm in the change that was taking place in this Western land that was his heritage.

For this was August of the year 1850, the second season of the great California Rush. Another thirty thousand stampeders had gone through Independence earlier in the year, and the bulk of them were far beyond South Pass by now, strung out along the Humboldt, toiling and quarreling and dying in the race to the promised land.

Luke had first encountered the litter and the squander of their passing at Fort Laramie on the Platte when he had come out of the Teton country with his string of ponies bearing his winter's catch.

The scar lay across the face of the plains like an offense, miles wide and endless in its length. Grass eaten to the roots and the roots ground into powder in the soil by wheels and hooves. Every clump of sagebrush and hummock of grass festooned with abandoned rags and scraps of paper. Broken, deserted wagons tilted drunkenly in the stream crossings. The scant timber along the fords wiped out, and the carcasses of unwanted buffalo that had been slain merely for the sake of marksmanship festering in the sun.

And all the tribes on the plains sullen and set on a hair trigger at this despoiling of their land.

It was even worse here in Independence. Luke felt stifled. He was in a cage. The place had tripled in size, then doubled again since his last visit. The two little taverns, where men like himself had clicked pewter mugs and drunk their mulled wine and buttered rum in comfort in the past, were now gone. Even their locations were unrecognizable amid the bawdy gambling houses and drinking traps. Other landmarks had crumbled beneath the human flood that had swept in from the alien land east of the Mississippi.

The speech of these intruders, their dress and their customs were foreign to him. He found himself a stranger in his own home — a home that stretched from here to the Pacific.

And so he shoved men aside. "Putty bellies!" he called them, hoping they would give him a chance to prove his strength over them.

The fact was that inwardly he was lonely and bewildered and frightened. Outwardly he was meeting this situation in the only way he knew — with loftiness and derision. For the sake of his pride, which was a vast and fearful burden, he would have endured the torture stake rather than give in to the desire to flee in a panic from this crowded, strange place.

The season was so late that the stampede was now recoiling upon itself. Many who had started were turning back and flowing homeward again through Independence rather than risk being caught by winter in the mountains. But others were still arriving from the East, by trail or steamboat, and milling around in the ceaseless, anxious debate that went on as to whether to attempt the long journey this year or wait until spring.

Some of the more daring ones had made up their minds. A company, Luke had heard, was pulling out in the morning, intending to try it by way of South Pass and the Humboldt River. Even now this outfit was holding its farewell party at the camp on the outskirts of town. As he wandered in their direction, there was scorn for them in his eyes — and a little pity too, for their foolhardiness. They were greenhorns, too inexperienced to know how high were the odds against them.

As he reached the outer fringe of the gathering a man had just finished offering a prayer. He was a preacher by his knee-length black coat and round hat. Angular and rawboned and touched by frost at the temples, he had the deeply seamed and weathered face of a man of stern principles. His hands were the big-knuckled, powerful implements of a man who knew what it meant to grip the handles of a plow. He stood on a wagon bed platform and prayed earnestly for divine guidance to carry the party through the dangers of the wild land that lay ahead.

Luke gazed around at the wide circle of

wagons that stood loaded and ready, their hoods of white drill unsullied and taut on the bows. He marked out four heavy freighters that stood together. These wagons each bore a designation lettered in bold black paint on their canvas:

MENAFEE TRADING COMPANY
TRACY MENAFEE, PROP.

Luke turned to bystanders and grinned knowingly. "The parson has got his sights set a mite high," he remarked. "If Tracy Menafee is mixed up in this then the preacher would have better luck, most likely, if he soft-soaped the Devil a little. Nothin' like havin' an extra string fer your bow."

Faces turned toward him, shocked and resentful. "Blasphemy!" an angular woman in calico said scathingly, and drew away from him, her lips pursed.

Luke's words had carried — as he had intended — to the group of roughly dressed men who lounged, smoking pipes, in the shadow of the Menafee Trading Company wagons. One of them, a man with thin, hard, dark features, who wore a holstered pistol, got to his feet, peering. Then he motioned two others to follow, and began circling through the camp in Luke's direction.

On the platform alongside the parson stood a kindly faced woman who evidently was his wife, and a girl. Both wore severe gray dresses and poke bonnets. The girl now seated herself at a big gilded harp and struck a chord. She began singing a camp meeting hymn to the strains of the harp. The elder woman joined in.

Luke laughed and lifted his voice in a jeering imitation of a coyote's lament.

The singers faltered. The girl, upset, struck a discord on the harp. She arose, gazing furiously in his direction.

"You — you vulgar, insulting ruffian!" she exploded.

"Never mind, dear!" the woman remonstrated.

"Proceed, Abigail," the minister commanded. "Proceed with the music!"

The girl seated herself angrily and drew her fingers forcefully across the strings of the harp. But it was no hymn that she played. It was the refrain of an army ballad, challenging and defiant. The minister glanced helplessly at his wife and shrugged.

"That's better," Luke said approvingly. "Folks want to be gay an' kick up their heels tonight. There'll be plenty of time for hymns an' preachin' later on. An' they'll be more needed, I tell you now."

The woman in calico changed her mind and came back to face him again. "What was that you said about the Devil, mister?" she asked apprehensively. "I'm Carrie Philips. My husband an' his brother own one of these wagons. We're Ohio folk. You seem to think we're in for trouble. Don't you figger we can make it to California this year?"

"Maybe," Luke said. "But you'd have a better chance if you headed for Santa Fe, then followed the old trappers' trail down the Gila by way o' the Pima villages an' across the California desert to San Diego, or to a pueblo called Los Angeles. You won't hit too much snow on that trip, but it won't be easy."

"But that's hundreds of miles farther," the woman protested. "They told us we could make it by way of the South Pass trail without trouble."

"Who told you?"

"Why — why, Trace Menafee."

"Figure it out for yourself, ma'am," Luke said. "It's already past midsummer. Even with the best o' luck it's three months' trip to the big mountains, the Sierra Nevadas.

Did Menafee tell you about them? That's the last range you got to climb to get to California. They're plenty high. They poke holes in the clouds. It'll be snowin' up there, most likely, by late October. Snow such as you never saw before. Ever hear of an outfit called the Donner party?"

A chill came over the listeners. The fate of that wagon company, which had been trapped in the mountain snows a few seasons earlier, was common knowledge.

"But Tracy Menafee says we can winter at Fort Relief on Raft River if it looks bad ahead," a man argued.

Luke's glance swung around the circle of wagons. "That would be right nice for Menafee," he said. "Did he mention that he owns Fort Relief an' that it's a trading post which he operates for profit? He'll sell you beans an' flour at a —"

He turned. The sinewy, dark-faced man stood there, backed by a slovenly, broken-toothed younger man and a huge, shaggy-haired, unshaven bullwhacker.

Luke said easily, "Howdy, Al. I noticed you and your pals when you first started to flank me."

Al Thorne answered in the same casual manner. "Hello, Luke. I heard you had hit town."

Al Thorne was wagon boss for Tracy Menafee. The impervious, unyielding hardness of obsidian was in him. He had killed men with the pistol he wore. It was said he had slashed one opponent to death with a blacksnake whip. He had beaten tough men with his fists. These qualities had made him important to Menafee. And authority had given him arrogance.

He spoke smilingly to the bystanders. "Luke has been drinking a little too much forty-rod," he said. "He likes to tell it spooky to women and kids."

"As I was sayin'," Luke remarked, "Tracy Menafee would be happy to sell beans an' flour at a dollar a pound to folks who have to winter at his post. O' course he'd mix in gravel an' sawdust to string out the supply, an' —"

The broken-toothed man had sidled aside so that he was partly behind Luke. He called himself the Missouri Kid. He wore the butternut shirt, striped breeches and hide boots of a wagonman, but he was, in fact, a product of the slums of cities, a pickpocket, a sneakthief and a fugitive from jail workhouses.

He leaped now, intending to alight on Luke's back and gain a garroting grip that could snap a man's neck or force him to beg for mercy.

Luke turned, lashing out with an upward-driven fist that caught this opponent in the stomach and in mid-air. The Kid's body was jackknifed by the force of that punch. He was limp before he struck the ground. There he lay doubled in agony, his lungs pumping futilely for breath.

Al Thorne and the immense whiskered man, who was known as Mack Sledge, had started to close in. But Luke's violence in disposing of the Missouri Kid startled them. They pulled up. Luke stood ready to move in any direction, awaiting their next decision.

Now the rawboned preacher, who had left the platform at a run, came charging between them. He pushed Thorne and Mack Sledge back.

"Peace! Peace!" he thundered. "Easy, Mr. Thorne! Easy! Let us not mar this evening, of all evenings, with strife. This man is not responsible for his actions."

He gazed at Luke, his brows fierce. "Your presence here is intolerable, sir," he said in his booming voice. "I am Emery Dixon, ordained minister of the Gospel, journeying with my devoted wife and niece to San Francisco, on my way to establish a mission on the Sandwich Islands. I advise you to leave before I find it necessary to have you taken to the lockup to sober up."

"That," Luke said, "might need some takin', parson."

The girl who had been playing the harp now came pushing through the circle. "Go away, you drunken troublemaker!" she raged. "You're spoiling the party."

Luke eyed her admiringly. "Now, danged if you ain't about as purty a piece o' calico as this child ever laid eyes on," he declared. "An' with plenty o' powder an' flint in your makeup. I can see thet you're meant for dancin' rather than singin' psalms an' twangin' on thet overgrown zither."

"If I were a man I'd beat that overbearing grin off your face," the girl said furiously.

"Abigail!" the preacher roared. "Go back to your aunt. You're making a spectacle of yourself."

Abbie tried to wither Luke with her big, angry Celt-gray eyes. He wouldn't wither.

"Oh, you — you — !" Words failed her. She whirled and walked away. Even in the severe gray dress and poke bonnet she was decidedly comely. And impetuous. Hair of a rich, deep golden brown showed beneath the bonnet. She was not much more than shoulder high to Luke, but what there was of her was quite sufficient.

Luke glanced down at the Missouri Kid who was beginning to revive a trifle, turned his back on Al Thorne and the minister, and shouldered his way through the circle and out of the camp.

His stride was still long and disdainful, and he carried himself with a swagger. But the liquor he had drunk was dead and frigid in his veins, and there was only dull apathy in his mind. He had shown his scorn of these aliens, and had demonstrated to his own satisfaction that he could master them physically. But in his heart he knew that he had proved nothing. He was like a man shouting against the wind, a man trying to stem a flood with his outspread fingers. He was fighting a lost cause. He was lonely.

He had had his fling. He meant now to head back to the plains — to Henry's Fork where he likely would hook up with others of his kind bound into the mountains for the winter. Or he might swing down to Taos and Santa Fe. Or strike direct for upper Green River. Maybe even for the forks of the Missouri in the Blackfoot country. Anywhere. It didn't matter.

A woman's figure moved out of the darkness as he rounded into the principal street, confronting him.

"Mr. Storm!" Ellen Jessup murmured. "Just a moment. I want a word with you."

"You're wastin' your time, little one," he said, and continued walking. "My dinero is about all gone."

Ellen kept pace with him, forced to hurry to match his swinging stride. She caught his arm. "You misunderstand," she said. "I am not what you think. This is important. This can be profitable to you."

They had reached a point where they were touched by the feeble glow of a lamp that had been left burning in a shop. Luke saw that she was young and seemed to be somewhat attractive, though in a brassy way.

He tried to free himself from her grasp. In the next moment he felt strong fingers close on his shoulder. He was swung forcibly around by someone who had stepped out of the darkness nearby.

"Is this fellow annoying you, ma'am?" a man said.

The girl, startled, released his arm. Luke's backlash was instinctive — and devastatingly swift. He spun, weaving low, prepared to meet any type of attack. His pistol was in his hand, and cocked, all in that one darting movement.

He had expected Al Thorne and his wagon men again. Instead he found himself gazing at a stranger.

The intruder had been taken by surprise by Luke's violent reaction. He stood eying the gun. There was more of annoyance than apprehension in his manner, as though he was condemning himself for not anticipating this move. He seemed to be about Luke's own age and nearly as tall. He had dark eyes in a handsome, intelligent face. His dark gray walking suit was quiet, but stylishly cut. He wore a pleated white shirt and a string tie and a cloth top hat in the fashion of the day, and carried a carved walking stick.

Luke now recalled that when he had been making his rounds of the taverns, he had noticed this good-looking Easterner playing poker in a game where the stakes had been steep.

The girl now tried to push Luke's gun down. "No! No!" she gasped. "No shooting! Please!"

The stranger ignored the pistol. He said wryly, "Perhaps I was wrong, ma'am. But I had the impression that this man was trying to force himself upon you."

"Why — why, not exactly," she stammered. "But — but, thank you anyway. I am in no danger, I assure you."

Luke straightened. He thrust the pistol back into his belt and began to grin cynically. "Maybe I was the one that needed help."

Dry amusement now showed briefly in the other man as he took Ellen's tawdry jewelry and her attire. Then his manner became punctiliously courteous. "Could I perhaps escort you to your friends, ma'am?" he offered. "My name is Cameron. Vance Cameron. I am a stranger in Independence. I arrived only late yesterday."

Ellen hesitated. She feared that the gray-haired man would appear any moment and she did not want to be seen talking to Luke. She accepted Vance Cameron's arm. "Thank you," she said. "I am staying at the Overland Inn."

Cameron looked at Luke. "You are fast on the draw, my friend," he observed almost admiringly. "You had me dead to rights and it was my own fault. I saw you handle that fellow at the wagon camp a few minutes ago. You are not as drunk as you should be. I noticed you several times during the day when you were making the rounds. I must say that you carry your liquor well. The next time I will not be as careless."

"Any time," Luke said magnanimously. "Any time at all."

Ellen said nothing. As she and Cameron turned away, her reticule slipped from her arm and fell to the ground.

When Cameron stooped to retrieve it she swiftly thrust an envelope into Luke's hand. Luke accepted the paper automatically and thrust it inside his hunting shirt before Cameron straightened and returned the reticule to its owner.

Chapter III

Luke watched Vance Cameron escort the girl away. He looked down at his own garb — the beaded hunting shirt, the flamboyant sash, the charro breeches and flashy moccasins. Beneath his shirt a medicine sack hung against his skin as a charm against bullets and arrows — and civilization. As an added protection a Shoshone medicine man had tattooed another mystic sign above his heart.

He finally drew out the message the girl had forced upon him. But the light here was too uncertain for reading. He made his way into the heart of the town, entered a tavern and ordered a mug of ale at the bar. This he carried to a table in a far corner where he had a measure of privacy.

He held the message below the table top out of sight of other eyes, for the manner in which it had been delivered clearly indicated a desire for secrecy. The words, written in an educated feminine hand, were terse:

I have a matter to discuss that might interest you. Please inquire at Room 16, Overland Inn, at your earliest convenience this evening. I would prefer that our discussion be entirely private.

That was all. There was no signature. Nor was his own name mentioned. Luke was somewhat deflated by the business-like tone of the epistle. He had expected something else. His first impulse was to destroy the paper and forget the whole thing. He did tear the message into fragments and grind them into the sawdust beneath his moccasins. Ignoring the affair was another matter. There was a mystery in all this that nettled and intrigued him.

He left his drink untasted, for alcohol held no further zest for him for this day at least, and strolled to the Overland Inn. The clerk's office was set off by a wooden partition from the main room where the gambling and drinking was going on.

A dog-eared register lay on the plank counter. There was the customary pigeonhole rack on the wall for keys and messages. A stairway at the rear mounted to the lodgings on the second floor.

The clerk was absent at the moment. Luke scanned the penciled names on the register, each with the room number inked in. He had to turn back a page until he found the one he sought. Room 16.

The name written there was "Mrs. Edward Jarrett, Cincinnati, Ohio." The date of her arrival was three days ago. The penmanship of the signature was the same as that on the note she had handed him.

"Hell's little blue fishes!" Luke grumbled. "A married susie!"

He again decided to put the whole thing out of his mind. He left the Overland Inn and headed in the direction of the livery where his horse awaited. But, as he crossed the street to the opposite sidewalk, a man's voice called his name. "You there, Storm. I want a word with you."

The speaker stood in the lighted door of an office which was part of a big frame-built warehouse whose bulk fronted on the street.

Luke said evenly, "Howdy, Menafee."

"Come in, come in, Luke," Tracy Menafee urged. "Al Thorne just rode in from the wagons and told me you had a misunderstanding with some of my boys a while ago."

Luke hesitated a moment. This was a warning and also a challenge. The former he could comprehend, because he knew

Menafee, having had dealings with him in the past. It was the challenge that he could not ignore.

He said, "We all savvied each other well enough, Tracy."

And he walked into Tracy Menafee's office. There was a varnished counter, equipped with inkwells and quills, and desks and a ledger table and a big iron safe with a painting of Niagara Falls done in gilt and green on its door. The bookkeeper's tall stool was vacant at this hour of the evening, but, to the left, a door opened into the trading room where two clerks were still busy with customers. Tracy Menafee's trading and mercantile business was prospering.

Menafee slapped him on the shoulder in a very affable manner, led him through the swing gate into the desk enclosure and motioned him to a chair, then seated himself at a big golden-oak desk where business papers stood in precise order.

Menafee brought out a humidor of fine Cuban cigars and offered it. When Luke shook his head, the trader selected a smoke for himself, savored the bouquet for a moment, then chopped the end with a mechanical clip that stood on the desk. He lighted the cigar from the burning taper that floated in a jar of wax, and leaned back, puffing with satisfaction.

Menafee was a full-bodied, sizable man who had a round, ruddy face with a studied bland expression. He had started out as a boy in the keelboats, helping cordelle the craft up the Missouri River by manpower in the last days of the big fur companies. The iron of that brutal form of physical slavery was still in his muscles — and also in his mind. Now, with softer living, he was fattening at the jowels and neck and middle. But there the softness ended.

After twenty-five years of great effort he was head of his own freighting and trading company. He wore expensive garb and a diamond ring. His thin brown hair was neatly barbered and he smelled of bay rum and cologne. Always fastidious of his appearance, he was clean-shaven and had a scrubbed look. Only his small hazel eyes were pallid.

Al Thorne stepped into the room from a rear door that opened into Menafee's private inner office. Luke wondered how many more of Menafee's men were beyond that door.

"I hear you're leaving Independence, Luke," Menafee said easily. He added, "Tonight."

And he dropped half a dozen gold pieces on the desk within Luke's reach. He said, "If you need credit for an outfit you're welcome."

"Tracy," Luke said, "you never was much good at handling anything but oxen and mules. When will you learn that there's a time for layin' on the whip, an' a time for givin' a horse — or a man — his head? Now, you've spoiled it. Fact is, I was headin' for Jake Adams' livery to catch up my horse and hit the trail west. Now, I've got to stay."

Al Thorne spoke. "If you stay you'll keep your mouth shut — one way or another."

"Let me do the talking, Al," Menafee snapped. He looked at Luke and was even-mannered again. "I would appreciate it, Luke," he said, "if you would not try to frighten those people in the wagon company. After all, they're not children. They know what they're doing."

Luke's brows lifted. "Do they now? Why I sized 'em up as a bunch of greenies. Do they know they'll be scratchin' for graze for their stock all the way from the Nebraska bluffs to the finish — wherever the finish is? Do they know that the Sioux Nation is movin' down to the Medicine Road an' beginnin' to act ugly? I passed the places where two small wagon outfits had been done in. It was just beyond the South Platte ford. Nothin' left but wagon tires an' ashes. Do they know —"

Menafee's patience broke. "You went out of your way to make some wild accusations against me personally," he exploded. "Just because you and I have had differences in the past is no reason for trying to cause confusion among these people now. They are organized and determined. I warn you to mind your own business."

Luke shrugged. "There you go ag'in, Tracy. Usin' the whip an' the goad. You'll never learn." He turned toward the door. "But you're right on one count," he added. "Those boomers are old enough to be able to figure things out for themselves. If they can't, I reckon it's their bad luck."

"See that it isn't yours, Luke," Menafee called after him as he left the office.

Menafee jammed his cigar savagely into an ash tray, snapping it and crushing it. He had made a mistake in threatening Luke and knew it. He did not like to make errors in Al Thorne's presence. He could see the sardonic amusement in Thorne's sharp eyes. Thorne was ambitious. He was already considering himself as more than Menafee's wagonmaster. He was smart, and he was also a man of dangerous impulses.

The knotty-jawed Missouri Kid now joined them, entering from the inner office. "Do we foller him an' take care of him?" he whispered eagerly.

Menafee glared at him with some distaste. "No!" he growled. "Let him go. He won't do any more harm."

The Missouri Kid was still green around the lips from the effects of the devastating body punch Luke had dealt him at the wagon camp. "You mean you're goin' to let him git away that easy?" he demanded angrily. He touched a sheathed knife that he carried hidden beneath his shirt. "I promised myself I'd cut off his damned ears."

Menafee's scowl deepened. The Missouri Kid was not one for neatness. His boots were squashed and run over at the heels. One leg of his wrinkled breeches was stuffed partly in a boot top. The other flapped free. He was unwashed, his crooked face patched with an uncertain growth of pale reddish beard. He offended Menafee's desire for refinement. It was Menafee's regret that he must depend on such persons for his purposes.

"Not in this town," he said. "Settle your grudges some other time and somewhere else. That's an order. I want no more trouble until this wagon company gets out of —"

He broke off. A newcomer had appeared in the door from the street, and stood there, tentatively awaiting an invitation. It was the heavy-bodied, gray-haired man whom Ellen had evaded earlier in the evening.

"Mr. Menafee?" he inquired.

"Yes," Menafee said. "I'm Tracy Menafee. What can I do for you?"

"My name is Slater," the man said. "Dan Slater. From Pennsylvania. I hear you've got a string of wagons pulling out for the plains with the company tomorrow. I'm planning on going to California myself, and would like to make a deal with you."

"Deal? Of what nature?"

"I'm alone," Dan Slater explained. "I want to hook up with a wagon where I'd be sure of food and shelter."

Seeing the refusal forming in Menafee's face he added quickly, "I'm able to pay, of course — enough to make it worth your while."

Menafee became interested. He never turned down a chance to earn a profit, large or small. "We're not in the business of carrying passengers, of course," he said.

"And my wagons are bound only as far as Fort Relief on Raft River. You say you are aiming for California. However I might send a wagon or two all the way, depending on circumstances."

"I guess it isn't much farther to California if I can make it to Fort Relief," Slater said. "I'd be willing to take my chances."

Menafee and Al Thorne smiled a little at that. It was very evident that the applicant knew nothing about the vast distances of the journey he was proposing.

Menafee appraised Dan Slater's garb and manner, trying to estimate just how high he dared go in setting the fare.

"We might make a concession," he said. "This is my wagon boss, Al Thorne. I imagine we could take care of this gentleman during the trip, Al. Mr. Slater, you look like you'd be good company on such a journey, sir. It happens that I'm traveling with my wagons, as I want to look after my affairs at Fort Relief. Let me see. I imagine that about one hundred dollars fare, and two dollars a day in addition for board and keep, would be sufficient."

Dan Slater studied it over. Finally he nodded. "It's higher than I had expected," he said. "But I'll accept. I have bank drafts and letters of credit that I'm sure you'll find satisfactory. What will I need in the way of equipment?"

Menafee named off some of the items. "We have them all for sale in the store. My clerks will advise you. You can buy everything you need tonight."

He added, "And I'd advise taking two good rifles and plenty of ammunition. And at least one pistol. There'll be good sport with buffalo and antelope, of course, but there is also always the chance of a brush with Indians, you understand."

"Yes," Dan Slater said. "Shooting is one department, at least, in which I can hold up my end."

They shook hands. Dan Slater moved toward the door leading to the trading room, then paused.

"I noticed you conferring with a young lady at your wagon yard today," he said. "She seemed to be buying a wagon and a team of oxen. I have noticed that she is staying at the Overland Inn, where I'm putting up, and that she seems to be alone. I admit that it's none of my affair, but I am curious. Surely a lone young lady isn't fixing to make the trip with her own wagon?"

Menafee smiled indulgently. "That

would be Mrs. Jarrett." He nodded. "Mrs. Edward Jarrett. She's got a husband in the California mines who evidently has struck it rich. She's in a hurry to join him." He laughed and winked. "I suspect she's afraid one of those pretty California señoritas will steal him away from her. She intends to hire a driver to take care of her wagon and stock and ride to California in style."

"She must be a game one," Dan Slater said. "Well, it encourages me. If a young lady has the sand to tackle a trip like that I guess I can make it too."

"We pull out at daybreak," Menafee said. "I'll send one of my men to call you in time, if you wish. The Overland Inn, you say?"

"That's it." Dan Slater nodded. "Room Number 20." And he walked into the trading store to start his buying.

Menafee looked at Al Thorne and the Missouri Kid. "What do you make of him?" he murmured.

"John Law," Thorne said softly.

"It sticks out all over him," the Missouri Kid spat. "A cussed, square-toed bullhead. Hell, I kin smell 'em a mile upwind. He's got a law badge pinned on him somewhere."

"I came to the same conclusion," Menafee said.

"What's he doin' here?" the Kid muttered, his cloudy eyes uneasy.

"I doubt that he is interested in you, my friend," Menafee said contemptuously. "He is an Easterner. A Pennsylvanian, he said. However, I detected a certain accent that reminded me of a man I knew who was from New York City."

He sat pondering a moment. "It's my guess that he is dogging someone whose destination he doesn't know. This decision to cross the plains evidently was forced upon him suddenly. No man would come here so unprepared if that was what he had in mind originally. Apparently he has a generous expense account. He didn't quibble over the price I asked. That means the matter involved is no petty affair."

He lighted a fresh cigar while he thought over the interest Dan Slater had shown in the young woman who had bought a prairie wagon and four yoke of oxen from him at his corrals that morning. Menafee had also been intrigued by Mrs. Edward Jarrett and her purchase and had puzzled over the matter frequently during the day. He had asked a price far above what the wagon and cattle were worth. Like Dan Slater, she had not bothered to haggle. She had paid promptly in cash. He had gained the elusive impression that her reasons for seeking to find her husband in California were far more urgent than she wanted anyone to know.

He rose and moved to where he could peer into the trading room. There were four or five patrons, and the clerks were occupied. Dan Slater stood, packing a brier pipe, awaiting his turn.

"Go in there, Al," Menafee murmured. "Keep Slater there as long as possible. Then take him to a tavern and buy him a drink or two." He turned to the Missouri Kid. "And you," he whispered, "slip over to the Overland Inn and take a look at his room. Number 20. Maybe we can find something in his luggage that will tell us more about him. Use the back stairs. Make sure you're not seen. You won't have any trouble breaking into the room?"

The Missouri Kid showed his crooked yellow teeth in a grin. "I got keys that'll open any door in the place."

"You've probably already visited rooms there when the guests were absent," Menafee sniffed. "Hustle now. We'll keep Slater occupied for half an hour or so."

The Missouri Kid left by way of the rear office into the dark wagon yards at the rear. Al Thorne strolled into the trading room and joined Dan Slater, engaging him in conversation until they gained the attention of a clerk. Then Thorne made himself helpful with advice and careful selection in the purchasing.

The Missouri Kid was gone twenty minutes. Then he returned soundlessly and excitedly beckoned Menafee to join him in the rear office. Menafee carefully closed the door after him when he entered.

The Kid whispered triumphantly, "Cast your eyes over these things!" He thrust folded papers into Menafee's hands. "I found them hid inside a folded shirt in his valise! He's a lawman, like we figured. See what it says there in them black letters? That means 'Wanted For Murder,' don't it? I've seen a lot of them kind of posters. It's one of them reward dodgers they tack up in places. An' these other two papers are arrest warrants. I've seen them kind of things before too. Plenty of 'em."

Menafee stood gazing at the papers in his hand. The warrants had been issued in the city of Baltimore. The reward poster bore penciled notations. The amount offered was ten thousand dollars.

Menafee could feel his pulse pounding in his throat, but he managed to hold back any change of expression as he read the small print on the warrants and on the poster. He knew the Kid's knowledge of reading was exceedingly limited. He even forced a wry grimace of disappointment.

"Nice work," he said. "But it was a waste of time. This is all about a fellow named Henry Jones who is wanted for a killing in Pittsburgh. Evidently Slater has been trailing him."

He handed the papers back to the Kid. "Might as well put 'em back where you found them. Make sure you leave everything exactly as you found it. I wouldn't want our detective friend to know we went to the trouble of poking into his luggage. Make it fast."

The Missouri Kid was chagrined. "But why was the feller so interested in makin' sure that the gal was goin' west?" he demanded.

"I wouldn't know." Menafee shrugged.

The Kid started to debate the point, but when he saw Menafee's gaze turn cold, he thought better of it. With a shrug he pocketed the papers and left the room. Menafee surmised that he likely would take the time to try to decipher what he could of the printing on the documents. He might even arrive at the real gist of the matter. But that could not be helped.

Now that he was alone a wild excitement flamed in Menafee's wide face. Then a hand tapped the door. It was Al Thorne.

"Where's Slater?" Menafee gasped, alarmed.

"Still in the trading room, trying on boots. Don't worry. He's busy. I'll buy him a drink afterwards. Has the kid . . . ?"

Thorne paused, eying Menafee closely. Then he stepped through the door into the inner office and closed the portal behind him. "You've found something, Tracy," he murmured. "You look like you just picked up four aces."

"Al!" Menafee breathed. "Do you remember hearing about a banker back in Baltimore named Henry Jessup who slipped out with about two hundred thousand dollars of his depositors' money? It happened some weeks back."

"Yeah," Thorne nodded, thinking. "I read about it a few days ago in a newspaper that somebody, just in by steamboat from the East, had left at a barbershop. A killin' was mixed up in it. Seems like the daughter was in cahoots with her father an' they tried to frame the steal onto a bank clerk who was sweet on her. The clerk was rubbed out and —"

Thorne broke off. He gazed at Menafee

and the same excitement now began to build up in him.

"Exactly!" Menafee said. "This Mrs. Edward Jarrett didn't ring true from the first minute she came to the office to dicker for a trail wagon. She dresses like a hussy and poses as the wife of a get-rich prospector, but she forgets at times and talks and acts like she was born on a silver plate. And she seems to have money."

"Are you sure? How did you find out?"

"Dan Slater seems to be some kind of a law officer, right enough," Menafee said. "It's my guess he's a detective hired to work on the bank case. The Kid found papers in his luggage — warrants for the arrest of Henry Jessup and his daughter, Ellen Jessup. And a reward dodger that tells why they're wanted. The dodger carries descriptions of both of them. The description of Ellen Jessup fits Mrs. Edward Jarrett as tight as a pair of new silk stockings. There's no mistake. And ten thousand dollars' reward is being offered for their arrest and the recovery of the stolen money."

"But why is she headin' for California?" Thorne muttered.

"And why not? As I remember the accounts of the affair, Henry Jessup skipped before the body of the murdered clerk was found. It was not until then that they had any case against the lady. But she escaped from Baltimore before they could arrest her. My guess is that her father had already started for California and that she is on her way to meet him. With the mountains swarming with stampeders from all over the world the gold mines are an ideal spot for such persons to lose themselves, change their names and start life over again, pretending they made their stakes in the placers."

There was a silence. "Ten thousand reward!" Thorne said hungrily.

"Two hundred thousand!" Menafee murmured. "Why be pikers?"

They looked at each other. "Of course," Thorne said softly.

"We must keep close tab on the lady," Menafee said.

"How about the Kid? Does he know?"

Menafee shrugged. "He suspects. He can't read much, but he's shrewd enough to do some guessing."

"What's your plan, Tracy?"

"We'll accompany Mrs. Jarrett all the way to California, and take pains to see that she arrives there safely and as speedily as possible. It's her father we must find.

He's the one who will have the money. And she is the only person who can lead us to him."

"What about this Dan Slater?"

"Slater evidently intends to follow her with the same object in mind, and —"

Suddenly he remembered that Dan Slater had been left unwatched. With an exclamation he brushed past Thorne and hurried into the main office and peered into the trading room.

Dan Slater was not in sight.

"Mr. Slater will be back in a few minutes, Mr. Menafee," the clerk said in response to a snapped question. "He was not carrying enough cash with him to pay for his outfit and I imagine he went to wherever he is putting up to get more money."

Menafee whirled and looked at Al Thorne in consternation.

At that moment gunfire erupted somewhere in the town. Menafee rushed to the outer door. Excitement was boiling around the Overland Inn down the street.

Chapter IV

Luke had expected to be followed when he had walked out of Tracy Menafee's office. Menafee, for all his outward air of respectability, could be violently ruthless when crossed — particularly when the matter of profit in his business ventures was involved. And certainly the Missouri Kid was the kind who would yearn to pay him off for that stomach punch.

He moved down the street, then crossed swiftly to the opposite walk and returned to a point where, from the deep shadows beneath a store's wooden awning, he had a view through the open door into Menafee's outer office. The Missouri Kid had now joined Thorne and Menafee in the room. Presently a stocky stranger entered from the street and began talking to Menafee. Evidently some business matter was being discussed.

Satisfied that he had nothing to fear for the moment at least, Luke gave up his vigil and moved away.

His thoughts now returned to the message the young woman had handed him during the encounter with Vance Cameron. He argued with himself that his first hunch had been correct and that she must be a fandango girl. He had been prodigal with his money and she probably imagined that he was still in funds. He laughed wryly and his fingers touched the buckskin poke that hung inside his shirt below the medicine sack. It was very slim.

Still . . . a nagging curiosity tugged at him. There were tantalizing questions that kept arising in his thoughts in regard to this Mrs. Edward Jarrett. He remembered the way she carried herself. Straight and high-chinned as though she considered herself a cut above the common run. And her manner of talking during the excitement when she had tried to intervene in his clash with Cameron had been in contrast to the cheap adornment she wore.

Luke headed directly for the Overland Inn, suddenly resolving to settle, once and for all, the matter of Mrs. Edward Jarrett and her message. Remembering her apparent assurance that he would be glad to obey her summons, he let hostility rise within him.

Reaching the Overland Inn, he strode through the tavern and mounted the stairs. He found himself in a barren hallway whose only light came from a bracket lamp which hung near an open door at the rear. The door led to the platform of an outside stairway.

Treading the dry boards, he finally came to a door which bore the number he sought — 16. Lamplight showed at the threshold. He tapped peremptorily on the panel.

A woman's voice sounded. "Who is it?"

"Luke Storm," he answered tartly. "Or was you maybe expectin' others?"

The bolt was freed and the door opened. She motioned him in and murmured, "Please keep your voice down. These walls are thin."

She quickly bolted the door after he had entered. He looked her over. She had removed the bonnet and jacket. He saw now that she was younger than he had thought — and decidedly more attractive. Her hair and eyes were very dark, her skin fair and clear, her features finely cut. She was slim of waist and throat, but was well-endowed with curving grace at other points. She had removed the dangling earrings and tawdry bracelet and had rubbed the rouge and powder from her face. That made quite a difference.

Grinning a little, Luke moved toward her. "You went to a lot o' trouble to bring me up here, little one," he said. "I —"

She backed away from him. There was no fear in her, Luke saw. Her reticule stood on the bed, and now she lifted her pistol from it.

She did not point the weapon, but merely stood with it hanging at her side. "I can understand that you may have gained the wrong impression of me," she said levelly. "I do not blame you. However, I must make it clear that I will never condone an attempt at familiarity, no matter what the circumstances, or how close our association might be. I will shoot if you make this error again."

Luke had one answer at least. She was no harlot. He found that discovery invigorating, even though her self-assured manner further rubbed against the grain.

"You won't need the gun," he said. "It wouldn't stop me anyway. What was that you said about us bein' in close association? I didn't savvy."

She studied him a moment, then returned the pistol to the reticule. "First," she said, "I have a question or two. I heard what you said at the wagon camp tonight. You don't seem to think there is too good a chance of getting through to the gold mines this season by the South Pass route."

"It can be done, but they'll have to move mighty fast an' be lucky," Luke said.

"You made a remark about Tracy Menafee. You implied that he had some underhanded intention in this matter."

"Danged if you don't use long-handled words," Luke snorted. "I wasn't implyin', as you put it. I was sayin' it straight an' plain enough."

"I stand corrected," she said. "At least you are frank. That is one point in your favor."

Luke gazed at her smokily. He felt that he was being appraised as one would study a horse that was to be bought. "I'm sound o' wind an' limb too, Mrs. Jarrett," he drawled. "Want to look at my teeth?"

Ellen smiled coolly. "So you know my name?"

"Looked it up on the book at the desk."

"Mr. Menafee insists that the company will make it to California ahead of winter. Why is he so positive, if you consider it such a risk?"

"Menafee's a businessman," Luke said.

"He'd skin a gnat for its coat. He skinned me once when I had to sell him my year's trap o' furs for enough grub to keep from starvin'. Right now he owns a tradin' post called Fort Relief out in the Shoshone country. It's near the fork o' the Oregon and California trails. He makes his money off stampeders."

"I'm beginning to see your point," Ellen said.

"Fort Relief is just a little more'n halfway to everywhere an' nowhere," Luke told her. "It's where immigrants start runnin' low on grub an' their cattle an' horses are givin' out. They're growin' mighty scared. Menafee sells 'em stock that he's taken in trade on his own terms from other scared people an' freshened up a little. He sells food too — at prices that only a man with hungry kids an' womenfolk on his hands will pay."

"I understand," Ellen said.

"Menafee would like nothin' better'n to have twenty, thirty wagons of boomers marooned at his tradin' post all winter," Luke went on. "Come spring, he'd have every cent, every head of stock, every wagon they own."

He watched her consider this for a time before she spoke. "It happens that I am traveling with this wagon party," she said. "I can't afford to be marooned at Fort Relief or anywhere else. I must reach California this fall at all costs. Have you ever been over the trail?"

"Most of 'em, I reckon."

"Most of them?" she said incredulously. "How many?"

"I've made it by way o' the Pima villages an' the Gila River." Luke grimaced. "That's long travelin' through a devil's desert whar trees grow thorns instead o' leaves. I've been over the Spanish trail also, which is purely hell fer canyons an' mountains. I've traveled this South Pass too, an' have clumb the mountains the Californians call the Sierra Nevadas. They're as high as the big Rockies, an' in winter they look like big white tombstones waitin' fer you to die." His mind carried him back over those harsh distances. "Yeah," he said musingly, "I've been to California. I know all the trails. An' there is no easy one."

"I bought a wagon and eight oxen today," Ellen said. "Tracy Menafee also offered to find a driver for me. But I prefer to do my own hiring. I have you in mind. That's why I asked you to come here."

Luke glared at her. She was taken aback by the sudden storm in his face. "Me —

hire out as a bullwhacker?" he exploded. "Me — work for a female an' a snob at thet?"

He discovered that this dark-eyed girl could give him glare for glare. "Bullwhacking, as you call it, is honest work at least," she flashed. "But that would be only a part of your duties. The real reason I am offering you the position is that I intend to strike out for California by myself if the other wagons do not go through this season. In that event I will need a guide who knows the trail."

Luke backed off a pace and looked her over. He laughed scornfully. "Hell, ma'am!" he snorted. "You won't even tough it out as fur as the first Platte crossin'. You don't stack up like the kind that was meant for roughin' it. You're more in the habit o' being waited on, an' orderin' servants around, or I read your trail wrong."

For an instant he saw dismay in her eyes. "I'm certain that if a girl like Abbie Wallace can make it, then I can too. I do not believe she knows any more about roughing it than I do."

"Abbie Wallace?" Luke questioned.

"She's the missionary girl whose singing and harp playing you insulted with your wolf howling."

"Oh, her! Cute as a spotted pony, wasn't she? I reckon she might make it at that. Bein' a missionary, she'll have the Lord on her side. But who've you got?"

"You," Ellen said. "I'll pay a dollar a day."

Luke sniffed disdainfully. "Did I hear straight when you allowed thet you meant to strike out alone for California if the others decide they can't make it. Just you an' me?"

"Any others will be welcome to join us — if they can keep up," she said. "If not, then it will be the way you stated it." Her gaze met his steadily. She was not bothering to spell out stipulations, nor was she offering concessions.

"Danged if you ain't a bold one," Luke admitted. "Why are you in such a lather to get to the gold mines?"

"Not that it's any of your concern, but let us say I am anxious to join my husband there."

Luke glanced at the wedding band on her finger. Suddenly he was certain that this was no more a real part of her life than the garb she wore or the drab room in which they stood.

"I've got no yearnin' to go to California again," Luke said. "I'm sick of distance."

"Two dollars a day," she said. Then, seeing the look in his face, she added swiftly, "No! I'll put it another way. The way I really feel. I would appreciate it if you would help me, but not for pay alone."

"You've got a quick mind, ma'am," Luke said approvingly. "An' you learn to read people in a hurry, don't you? You're almost talking my language. But . . ." He turned toward the door. ". . . but I still don't hanker for the job of ridin' herd on a lone female greenhorn. You'll have to look somewhere else."

She accepted that as final. "Just a moment, please, until the hallway is vacant," she murmured. "I would prefer that no one learn a man had been in my room."

Luke waited, his hand on the knob, for heavy footsteps were approaching in the hallway. They passed on and a key rattled in a lock a few doors farther on.

That aroused a stunning burst of sound. First a startled shout, then the crash of two gunshots shook the flimsy building. The explosions were so near that Luke felt the jar inside his eardrums.

Running footfalls sped past the door in the direction of the stairway at the rear. They were followed by another uncertain pair of running feet. Luke heard the gasping, blood-strangled breathing of a man in agony.

Another gunshot crashed in the hall, the concussion rattling the door. Luke tugged frantically at the knob. The door would not open. He had forgotten that it was bolted. The bolt resisted for seconds. Then he finally got the door open.

The hall was fogged with powder smoke. A figure lay sprawled through the open outer door onto the platform of the rear stairway.

Luke stepped out and closed the door behind him. He walked down the hall and stood over the fallen man. It was the stocky, gray-haired stranger he had seen enter Tracy Menafee's office little more than half an hour earlier.

The man was dead in a spreading stain of crimson. He lay face down, one outstretched arm dangling over the outer edge of the platform, which was guarded only by an open wooden railing. Luke noticed that this hand held what appeared to be a few folded papers of the size of legal documents. Then the fingers released their grip and the papers fluttered downward into the darkness of the alleyway below.

Luke peered down the flight of stairs. Whoever had poured those bullets into the gray-haired man had reached ground level and fled into the shadows of the alley before Luke had arrived above.

Heads were now appearing cautiously at other doors along the hallway. And a flood of men came pounding up the inner stairs from the tavern below. Then all of them slowed to a stop and stood looking at Luke as he stood there in the lamplight on the outside platform with a dead man at his feet.

Luke realized for the first time that he had instinctively drawn his pistol when he emerged from the girl's room. He held it gripped in his hand, pointing downward. An uneasy premonition chilled him. It built up into consternation as he suddenly guessed what they were thinking.

Someone in the crowd said uneasily, "Better put down that shootin' piece, mister. You've done enough harm."

Vance Cameron came pushing roughly up the stairs and into the foreground. He pulled up, gazing at the gray-haired dead man, a horrified, shaken look forming in his face.

"Stand there, fellow," Luke said, "until we talk this over. I didn't kill this poor man. I don't even know who he is."

Tracy Menafee, followed by Al Thorne,

now came up the stairs, the other men making way respectfully for them. Menafee was breathing hard as though he had done some unaccustomed running. He pointed dramatically at Luke.

"Why, it's that drunken mountain man who's been hunting trouble all day," he exclaimed. "It looks like he's finally killed somebody. He should have been locked up long ago. Now he'll likely need hanging."

Vance Cameron spoke. "Lay down your gun, my friend. We want to take a look at it."

Luke was now remembering another factor that might help put a noose around his neck within minutes. His pistol had empty chambers. He was not sure how many. Two, at least. Perhaps three. For he had touched it off once or twice during the day, shooting in the air in the exuberance of his celebration. He had not bothered to go through the tedium of reloading the cap-and-ball weapon to its capacity.

"I've got empties in my gun," he said. "I did some poppin' when I was feeling happy. They were fired hours ago, but I couldn't prove it here in this place reekin' with fresh-burned gunpowder. It's my guess this fellow surprised a sneakthief in his room. The thief began shootin'. This man chased him down the hall, but he got clean away."

"Grab him, men!" Menafee ordered. "He's the sneak thief himself. The man he killed just bought a trail outfit at my trading store. He displayed his wallet. Luke Storm must have seen that, and followed him here to rob him."

Al Thorne took up the cue. "Lynch the cussed murderer!" he shouted. "Let's string him up."

Thorne led a surge of movement toward Luke. Luke had seen mobs form under just such sudden circumstances, seen them lynch men without trial or mercy and regret it later.

He moved back, but there was no escape. The outer stairway was by this time also jammed with arrivals who had come from the street by that route. He was trapped.

Then a woman's voice made itself heard above the shouting. "Wait! Wait! You are making a mistake!"

It was the dark-eyed young woman who called herself Mrs. Edward Jarrett, standing in the open doorway of her room.

Her cry brought a spreading silence. When she could make herself clearly heard she spoke again. "This man, Luke Storm, had absolutely nothing to do with the shooting. I can testify to that under oath."

"Why are you so sure, ma'am?" Vance Cameron asked.

She stood a trifle straighter, her chin lifted. Color came up from her throat and stained her cheeks. But her voice was composed. "Because he was here — in my room — when the shots were fired in the hall."

Nobody spoke for a moment. Then a drunken teamster in the front rank laughed knowingly. Luke moved forward and struck the man a teeth-jarring slap across the mouth.

He turned to Ellen. "That took spunk, Mrs. Jarrett," he said. "I reckon that everyone here now understands there was nothin' immodest about my bein' in your room. And I've changed my mind. On second thought I'll take the job you offered. I'll see to it that you get to California."

"Thank you," Ellen said.

Luke looked at Menafee and Al Thorne. "Any questions?" he asked.

The lynching mania had been cooled as swiftly as it had been incited. "Who am I to oppose a lady's word?" Menafee said. "My apologies, Mrs. Jarrett."

But Luke knew that, though all their

faces were now circumspectly blank, they shared the same viewpoint as the man he had chastised. And he was sure Ellen was aware of it also.

Now for the first time she had a clear view of the body on the stair platform. All the new color abruptly drained out of her features. She stood motionless, staring. Her gaze then came up to Luke, and moved onward over the faces of the bystanders as though numbly seeking an answer.

She said in a strange, shocked tone, "Oh . . . Oh!" Then she suddenly retreated into her room and closed the door. Luke heard the bolt slide into place.

An officious man wearing a constable's badge took charge. "I'll have some questions to ask you tomorrow when we hold the inquiry over the body," he told Luke.

Dan Slater's body was carried away on a stretcher. The hallway cleared as the crowd began to drift back to the tavern. Robbery and killings were no matter of lasting interest in this crowded, feverish town.

Luke's gaze stonily followed Menafee and Al Thorne as they descended the stairs. They avoided his eyes.

Vance Cameron lingered. Apparently he was less accustomed to scenes of violence and murder, for he looked pale. His dark eyes were moody.

"Menafee saw a chance to pay you off for those remarks you made about him tonight at the wagon camp," he said to Luke.

Luke eyed Cameron speculatively. "You know Tracy Menafee too?" he observed.

"I know only his type." Cameron shrugged. "But I happen to have a personal interest in this matter. You see, I have decided to head west with this company tomorrow, if I can arrange to join one of the wagons." He turned toward the stairs. "Good night, Storm. If I were you, I'd be mighty careful not to outline myself against lighted doors and windows tonight. You've bruised the feelings of several very unpredictable persons lately."

He started down the stairs. "And beware of women who pass secret messages to you on dark streets," he murmured. "That kind usually are using a man only for their own purposes."

He vanished below then. Luke stood frowning. Evidently Cameron had seen Mrs. Edward Jarrett hand him that written note. The fellow was not as ingenuous as he pretended.

Luke gazed speculatively at the bolted door of the dark-eyed girl's room. Then he too left the Inn. He made his way to a quiet tavern some distance away to kill some time. He had not forgotten the papers that had fallen from Dan Slater's dead hand into the darkness. He was waiting until the excitement had died down. Presently he strolled to the street. Making sure he was not being watched, he circled through back lanes and made his way to the rear of the Overland Inn.

The alley was deserted. There was no sign of activity in the hallway above the stairs. Evidently the constable had finished his investigation into Dan Slater's effects and had left.

The lamplight from the open door cast faint radiance over the rubbish heaps below, enabling Luke to find three folded slips of paper. With them in his hand he mounted the stairs to where he had better light for reading.

He stood staring at the same two warrants and the reward poster that Tracy Menafee had read earlier. A cold and growing horror worked through him. He again read the description of the young woman:

". . . very dark hair and eyes; about five feet, three inches in height; one hundred and eighteen pounds, exceedingly attractive. Ellen Marie Jessup is well-educated and intelligent. Has a pleasant speaking voice. Probably will attempt to hide in large cities."

There was no doubt about it. Mrs. Edward Jarrett was in reality a person named Ellen Marie Jessup who was wanted for connivance in the murder of her fiancé in Baltimore and the embezzlement of two hundred thousand dollars.

It was some time before Luke could move. It was like a punch to the heart. He finally thrust the papers inside his hunting shirt and made his way to the street.

The celebration at the wagon camp was ending and the singers were joining in a final song. It was one whose theme had become that of the great trail:

> "Oh! Susanna, Oh!
>   Don't you cry for me,
> I'm goin' to California
>   Some gold dust for to see."

The refrain drifted over the town. Luke could make out Abbie Wallace's voice, clear and high above all others. She sang the song with boisterous challenge. But

Luke sensed that there was no such certainty in the others. Already this wagon company was beset by doubt of its own destiny. California was far away and the season was late.

He walked to the livery, got his bedroll and spread his blankets in the hayloft. He lay pondering.

The pseudo Mrs. Edward Jarrett, whatever she might be, had saved him from lynchers. In doing so she had exposed herself to shame and disgrace. But, beyond that, she had risked disclosure of her true identity by facing so many men, for there was always the chance that in this boom town, crowded with travelers from every corner of the nation, there might be someone from Baltimore who would recognize her and warn the authorities. She had, in fact, chanced the gallows herself to speak for him.

Luke's independent spirit writhed. He resented obligation to anyone, least of all to a girl who seemed to look down upon him as though he were little more than an uncultured savage. But he could never bring himself to repay the favor she had done him by exposing her as a person wanted for murder.

He was pledged to see her safely to California. It was a promise given as lightly as though he had offered to escort her across the street. In reality it meant months of danger and privation, and perhaps death in mountain snows.

It also meant that he was helping her escape from the law. For it seemed clear to him now that this was why she had sought to hire him as a guide.

Chapter V

A perfunctory inquiry was held by town officials the next morning over the body of Dan Slater. Luke was the principal witness. He related what he had seen and heard, but did not mention the papers that had fallen from Slater's hand. He now had those papers hidden in his possible sack, along with his scant personal effects.

The inquiry was rushed to a quick conclusion. It was brought out that papers in Dan Slater's wallet identified him as an investigator connected with a well-known detective agency in the city of New York. He had letters of credit from a group of persons in Baltimore known as the Stockholders' Protective Association.

All this was an enigma to the men conducting the inquiry. Their verdict was: "Murder by a person or by persons unknown for purposes of robbery."

However, to Luke, the reason for Dan

Slater's presence in Independence seemed plain enough. No doubt Slater's letter of credit came from stockholders in the bank where the embezzlement had taken place, who had organized in an effort to track down the guilty ones in the hope of recovering some of their losses.

But Luke conceded that the verdict might be correct in naming robbery as the motive, and that the intruder in Slater's room might have no connection with the mission that had brought the detective west.

Still . . . why had those papers been in Dan Slater's hand when he had pursued the fleeing intruder down the hallway? Luke, from the sounds he had heard, believed Slater had struggled briefly with the man, and that he must have snatched the papers from his opponent during this first clash.

That brought up the possibility that the papers had been the real reason for the entrance into Slater's room. If this were not so, the intruder might simply have been reading the warrants when he was interrupted by the detective. In either case, the unknown person might be aware that the woman registered in that same inn as Mrs. Edward Jarrett was the Ellen Jessup who was wanted for murder. That would mean that her secret was shared by at least one other person in the town. And Luke wondered if there might be others. . . .

According to the reward poster, she was accused of luring a man named Ralph Gilmore, whom she was pledged to marry, into a trap where he had been murdered and the blame for the bank embezzlement placed on him.

An ugly crime. And now another murder, perhaps, could be written to that same account. For Luke was faced with the stark possibility that Ellen Jessup had had a hand in the killing of Dan Slater. Perhaps she was not as alone here in Independence as she pretended. Perhaps she had an accomplice who took care of such matters as Dan Slater's pursuit.

He kept remembering her reaction when she had seen Slater's body on the stair platform. Luke was certain she had recognized the detective. That meant she must have been aware that Slater had been trailing her. And the death of the detective had certainly been to her advantage.

Still . . . the horror and shock in her expression had seemed to be completely genuine. That hardly could have been the emotion of a person who had a hand in the killing.

Luke was caught between conflicting forces. It was his duty to turn her over to the law. But that was impossible, according to his stern code of honor, in view of the fact that he was indebted to her so gallingly.

He was at odds with everything she represented. She patronized him from her superior heights of breeding and education. Just as he had told her, she was accustomed to being waited on and to the softer things of life. But he had to grudgingly admit that she had displayed a considerable streak of grit, and also an utter indifference to her own personal safety when she had intervened to cool the lynching spirit that Tracy Menafee had aroused.

And the final truth was that Luke had little respect for the law as he had seen it represented at the inquiry or in the hallway of the Overland Inn.

Saddling his roan horse at the livery, he rode to the wagon camp. His possible sack was slung across the horse along with his tarp-covered bedroll. He carried rifle and pistol and there was a good supply of the best French powder and balls in the pouches at his belt.

He had stored away in his possible sack

the gaudy, beaded garb of his celebration the previous day. He had replaced his ragged buckskins with a new elkskin shirt and buckskin breeches and moccasins, that were unadorned and stiff with newness. The garments were of not too high a quality, and the fit left considerable to be desired, but he had been forced to hunt diligently to find even these articles, now that civilization had descended on Independence. Even so they were far more acceptable, in his viewpoint, than the wool and linsey and cowhide boots that were the commonplace garb of the boomers.

"These will have to do," he told the storekeeper sourly. "I'll raise myself a decent outfit first thing after I find me a 'Rapahoe or Cheyenne village where the squaws know how to tan hides proper an' chaw moccasin soles watertight."

Then, contrarily, he added white cotton shirts and heavy socks and underwear to his wardrobe — items that many mountain men would have scorned.

The caravan was waiting, the oxen standing idle in the growing heat. The people were gathered in the shade of the vehicles, talking in a stew of impatience. The sun was already mid-high in the morning sky.

Emery Dixon, the gangling missionary, was at the center of the largest group. Eyes turned curiously toward Luke, but without any real welcome. "Why didn't you boomers stretch out long ago?" he demanded as he rode up.

"Tracy Menafee said it would be better if we all started together," Emery Dixon said stiffly. "Mr. Menafee had to attend the hearing over the poor soul who was shot down in cold blood last night."

The Rev. Dixon's tone intimated that he held Luke responsible not only for the delay, but for Dan Slater's murder.

"Menafee could have caught up later," Luke said. "And so could I. You people would be three, four miles on your way by this time, if you had an ounce of sense instead of standing around like a flock of sheep waiting for someone to tell you what to do. Hear me now! Every mile — every minute — will count if you aim to make it to the mines this year."

"But Mr. Menafee is captain, and —"

"Who elected him?" Luke demanded.

"There has been no formal election as yet," Mr. Dixon said testily. "There seems to be no need for one. Tracy Menafee is eminently qualified for the position."

"It's customary to wait till a trail outfit

has made a few camps before it decides on its leaders," Luke said. "By that time even roundheads like you people will begin to know which way is directly up or down. That's the way it will be done in this outfit."

He stood up in the stirrups, peering up and down the waiting line of wagons.

Abbie Wallace spoke up. "Mrs. Jarrett's wagon is down that way, about third from the rear." She added, with a toss of her head, "So we're nothing but a bunch of roundheads? You evidently hold a very high opinion of your own intelligence, Mr. Storm?"

Luke grinned at her. "You're purtier in daylight even than in the dark," he said. "It takes a mighty comely gal to meet a test like that. But you want to take care o' that crop of long sorrel hair. There are Cheyenne an' Sioux an' Utes out where we're headin' that'd sell their chances of the Happy Land to own a long scalp like that." He added over his shoulder as he rode onward, "An' they'd rather have the gal than the scalp. Who wouldn't?"

He sighted Ellen standing beside a wagon near the end of the line. Her dark eyes lighted as he rode up, and he surmised that she had been worried, doubting that he would keep his word. She evidently had managed to increase her wardrobe. She wore quite a lot of clothes. Her full-skirted dress, underlain with petticoats and stays, would have been more in place at a garden party. A fetching poke bonnet, tied with green ribbons, was shading her face.

She too was more attractive in open daylight than he had expected. He decided that this, perhaps, was partly because she no longer wore the gaudy earrings and the rouge. Her face seemed more slim, more refined. She was a very fetching and alluring female.

She said, "Good morning, Mr. Storm!" and was careful to hide any apprehension his absence might have brought to her.

A huge man came into view from around the wagon and moved up. It was Mack Sledge, the bulking, shaggy-whiskered bullwhacker who had been with Al Thorne and the Missouri Kid the night before during the clash at the wagon camp party.

Luke dismounted. He looked at the wagon and the eight oxen in the yokes.

"This is the outfit I bought from Mr. Menafee," Ellen explained. "He had Mr. Sledge harness the oxen and take care of everything."

Mack Sledge grinned insolently. He had a

cud of tobacco in his loose-lipped face. He weighed two hundred and forty pounds and his shoulders were wide and sloping and thick with both muscle and fat. He had a reputation as a wrestler and had broken the ribs of more than one opponent. It was said that he could lift the wheel of a loaded prairie wagon clear of the ground. Sledge had been hoping he would inherit the chore of acting as driver for the fascinating Mrs. Edward Jarrett all the way across the plains. He resented Luke's last-minute appearance. And the defeat he and Al Thorne and the Missouri Kid had suffered at Luke's hands still rankled.

" 'Twon't be quite as cozy in the wagon as it was at the inn," he said with a knowing laugh. "But I reckon you two won't mind."

Ellen's mouth tightened, her dark eyes flashing angrily.

Sledge, a slow-witted man, hoped to goad Luke into a fight in which he could maim and cripple him so that Ellen would have to hire another driver. Sledge meant to be that person. He waited a moment, in anticipation. Then, when Luke gave no sign that he had noticed the insult, Sledge squirted tobacco juice and laughed ironically.

In the next instant, before he realized

what was coming, Luke was upon him in one long stride. An arm clamped about him, wheeling him, and he felt the sharp edge of Luke's hunting knife, chill and deadly, across his windpipe.

Sledge stood rigid, knowing that he was within a fraction of an inch from death.

"Take off your hat and tell the young lady that you are a filthy liar and that you humbly apologize," Luke said.

A tiny strand of blood began to show where he held the knife against Sledge's skin. The man's wide, loose face was the color of wet flour. He stood stiff and rigid, his eyes dilated as he visualized what the knife might do.

"Please!" Ellen cried. "I would prefer that you do not make an issue of the matter."

"Speak out, Sledge," Luke murmured inexorably. "The lady is waitin'. An' so am I."

"I 'pologize, lady," Sledge croaked. "I didn't mean nothin' ag'in yuh."

"All right," Luke said, and stepped back.

Faces were staring. Mack Sledge realized that dozens of wagon people had seen his abnegation.

Now that he was out of range of Luke's knife he tried to gather some of his reputation as a strong man around him. "Next time," he raged, "it'll be my turn! I'll bust you bone by bone. Arm by arm, an' leg by leg. Then I'll let you live — like a sick, crippled rabbit."

Luke sheathed his knife. "Let's settle it for keeps, here an' now, Sledge," he said.

Mack Sledge, the humiliation fevering his eyes, longed to take up the challenge. But as he gazed at Luke a doubt overcame the hunger. Sledge decided that this was not the time for him, nor the place. He turned away on his big, slapping feet and vanished among the wagons.

Someone had carried the news of the trouble to Emery Dixon. The missionary came hurrying to the scene. "You again," he said accusingly to Luke. "This is the second time you have engaged in violence in our midst, sir. I warn you that such conduct will no longer be tolerated."

Ellen spoke. "Mr. Storm had provocation on this occasion at least."

The missionary's gaze swung condemningly to her. "I can understand your interest in this man, madam," he said in his preaching voice. "This is the second time also that you have defended him lately. You at least are consistent — and loyal, Mrs. Jarrett."

His implication was plain enough. Ellen straightened. "I feel it is my duty always to defend anyone unjustly accused, Reverend," she said. "The Good Book says, 'Judge not, lest ye be judged.' "

"Perhaps it would be well to eliminate the Scriptures from this discussion," Emery Dixon said. "I understand that you are alone, Mrs. Jarrett, and that you have employed this man as your teamster. It is — shall we say — a very unconventional arrangement."

"What you are trying to say, Reverend," Ellen replied, "is that I am an immoral woman."

Emery Dixon had waded beyond his depth. He had not wanted to make an open accusation. But he was strong enough to meet the issue now that it was forced on him. "I neither condemn, nor do I judge. That is not for me."

Luke spoke. "But you throw a little mud around an' watch it smear things," he said. "You didn't have the right kind of bringin' up, parson. You try to find evil, when what you should be lookin' for is the sunshine."

Emery Dixon reddened and turned to the girl. "If you are ever in need of advice, Mrs. Jarrett, I will be at your service," he said hastily. Then he beat a retreat.

Luke watched Ellen's expression as she gazed after the departing minister. But he could not read her thoughts.

"Maybe I better find you another man to take care o' your stock an' wagon," he said slowly. "That would still their wicked tongues."

She turned and gazed at him quickly, searching. He saw the high pride and the defiance come back into her. And also the hurt. She forced a little smile.

"I care nothing about their talk," she said. "I am interested only in reaching California as soon as possible. I am depending on you to see that I get there."

"At least," Luke said approvingly, "you don't knuckle down to roundheads easy."

He resumed his inspection of her outfit. "The wagon's seen some hard use," he commented, "but it seems to be in fair shape. The oxen are not too bad. I've seen better. But they ought to make it as far as Menafee's fort with proper handling."

"You still think that Menafee is only interested in seeing that we winter at his trading post, don't you?" Ellen asked.

"He's already made a start in that direction," Luke observed. "Here 'tis, gittin' along toward noon, an' not a wheel turnin'. This won't be the last time this outfit will be delayed by Menafee an' his notions."

His words carried to nearby wagons. Men heard and stood uncertain and troubled.

"How old are you, ma'am?" Luke asked abruptly.

Ellen stared. Annoyance showed. Then she shrugged as though accepting a faintly amusing situation. "Twenty-four on my next birthday," she said. "Why do you ask?"

"I had decided last night you was maybe older," Luke said frankly. "You're smart in rubbin' off that paint an' powder an' gittin' rid o' the brass jewelry. Things like thet are for Piute squaws."

"Or loose women, you mean," Ellen said evenly.

The slap of trotting hooves sounded. Vance Cameron came riding up on a tough-mouthed, thick-bellied, black saddle horse. "Good morning, Mrs. Jarrett!" he said, lifting his hat. "Good morning, Storm! We are going to be fellow travelers. I've arranged to be attached to a wagon owned by one Mike McDuffy and his good wife." He slid from the horse. "It seems we are still being delayed," he went on. "Something to do with a broken fore-

hound on one of Tracy Menafee's freight wagons."

Luke uttered a snort. He leaped to a wagon hub and lifted his voice in a strident shout. "Let's roll! Those that can't move now, kin ketch up later. You there in the pilot wagons! Stretch out! Str——etch out!"

Chapter VI

That did it. A stir of excitement ran down the line of wagons. Men broke into action. They had been awaiting only leadership. Even the oxen aroused from their lethargy. Everyone — men and women and animals — faced westward — looked westward. Then a bullwhip cracked. A high-wheeled, canvas-hooded Conestoga wagon heaved into motion. Others followed.

A woman called wildly, "Goodbye, Missouri! Hello, California!" Then she burst into tears.

Guns exploded in the air. A bugle sounded. Banjos tinkled. The bell in the Independence courthouse began to toll. A churchbell joined in — the customary farewell to outbound caravans.

Near the head of the line Abbie Wallace stood in the bow of a wagon and her clear voice carried through the activity,

"Oh! Susannah, Oh! . . ."

Others took it up. The great song of the trail swelled loud and deliriously reckless. The die was cast now.

Luke picked up the coiled bullwhip from its hook on the wagon. Wagons ahead were all in motion.

Cameron turned to Ellen and helped her as she gathered her skirts and lightly mounted over the fore wheel and into the front bow of the wagon. Luke resented the dark-haired man's easy, well-bred manners. He popped the whip and the wagon fell into place in the column.

The song was rising higher from the throats of the others, but he noticed that Ellen was not joining in.

"They'd be smarter if they saved their singin' for a day when they'll be more in need of cheerin' up," he said.

"You seem to be positive there will be such days, Storm," Cameron remarked.

"I'm positive," Luke stated. He gazed at Cameron's stylish Eastern garb and then at Ellen's costume. He eyed her slim fingers, with their well-kept nails. Cameron's hands too, though not weak in appearance, were untanned and obviously those of a person unaccustomed to toil.

"You'll learn," he said. "You'll both learn."

"And you'll teach us, I imagine?" Cameron said, nettled.

"If I don't," Luke said, "the country will. An' you don't get a second lesson out there if you fail."

Cameron and Ellen traded glances and smiled a little. Cameron, on an impulse, tied his horse alongside Luke's sorrel which was on a halter rope at the tail of the wagon. Then he climbed into the wagon alongside Ellen.

"Your driver has a very poor opinion of me," he said.

"I'm afraid his estimate of me is no more flattering." Ellen smiled.

"I suspect that both of us are in for some trying times before we measure up to his standards," Cameron said.

Ellen's smile changed. It pushed Cameron away from her, closed all paths to her inner thoughts. "The truth is," she said, "that I have no desire to measure up to Mr. Storm's standards, as you put it. I am employing him as a teamster. Beyond that my interest in him ends."

"He interests me, however," Cameron said. "I've never encountered a person exactly like him. He is the only man I've met who seems to be utterly independent and sufficient unto himself. And he is also fearless evidently."

"His life has made him that way." Ellen shrugged. "He has lived by violence and ruthlessness. He is little more than an uneducated, brutal savage. No doubt he has taken scalps. Ugh!"

"No doubt," Cameron said. "And he will die by violence too, no doubt. And perhaps soon."

Ellen looked at him quickly.

"Storm has been stepping hard on Tracy Menafee's toes since he hit Independence. He just added further insult by prodding this outfit into action without Menafee's consent. Neither Mack Sledge nor the little rodent who is known as the Missouri Kid are the forgiving kind. He even made Al Thorne back down. From what I was told in Independence, Thorne is proud of his reputation as a gunfighter and killer." He was quiet a moment. "All in all," he concluded, "I wouldn't risk a penny on Storm's chances of living to see California."

Ellen was disturbed. "In that case I'll discharge him tonight at our first camp," she said, "for his own safety. If he leaves the wagon train he will be out of their reach."

"I have an idea that you'll find it difficult to discharge him," Cameron said. "I imagine he will suspect the reason. But speaking of Menafee, you're about to have him as a visitor."

Tracy Menafee was approaching, riding a blooded, red horse. Menafee was garbed for the trail in calico shirt, hard-twisted, striped breeches and boots. An expensive Panama hat shaded his ruddy, round face.

He gazed at Luke evenly as he rode up and said, "You stampeded 'em into pulling out, Storm. One of my wagons was not ready. After this the captain will set the time for moving."

"Daybreak will be the time for stretchin' out from now on," Luke said. "Any wagon that's not ready will be left behind — unless there's good reason."

"That," Menafee said, his pale eyes losing their affability, "will also be decided by the company officers. No man is going to control this caravan by frightening people into panicky action. It is all for one and one for all from now on. That is the only safety any of us will have on the plains."

He turned to Ellen and discovered that Cameron was in the wagon. He hesitated a moment, then smiled and lifted his hat. "Good morning, Mrs. Jarrett. And you, Cameron. I am at your service, Mrs.

Jarrett. Please feel free to call on me if there is anything I can do to add to your comfort."

He touched his hat again, then rode away to join his three wagons near the head of the column. His fourth wagon, which was said to be disabled, still stood on the camp ground, with Al Thorne and other men hurrying the repair work.

"A bid for your favor, and a warning to Storm," Cameron murmured to Ellen. "Menafee is not a subtle man. He did not appreciate finding me already occupying the place at your side. I am sure he intended to claim it for himself as a reward for acting as your champion."

"Champion?"

"Didn't you know that the Reverend Emery Dixon tried to call a camp meeting this morning with the intention of offering a motion to banish you and Luke Storm from membership in this company?" Cameron asked frankly.

Ellen winced. "Oh, no!"

"Menafee put a stop to it," Cameron said. "He made it plain that anyone attacking your reputation would have him to deal with. Or rather Al Thorne and the Missouri Kid and similar assorted ruffians who compose his crew, for Menafee would not soil his hands by chastising anyone personally if it could be avoided. He is now a respectable trader and hires others to do the rough work. At any rate no meeting was held. You are indebted to him for that."

He watched Ellen's expression. Evidently he found nothing in her face that answered whatever question was in his mind.

"You are a strange person," he said. "You might at least break into tears, or into angry defense of yourself."

"You are not a subtle man either, Mr. Cameron," Ellen said. "At least in this matter. What you are wondering is whether there really were romantic reasons for Luke Storm's presence in my room last night. You are not any more certain about my purity than Reverend Dixon."

"By Gad!" Cameron exploded admiringly. "You have a way of cutting a man down to size. No wonder Emery Dixon retreated in complete disorder."

He offered his hand. She hesitated. Then she placed her hand in his. "At least you are frank in your doubts of me," she said. "I appreciate frankness in anyone."

Cameron stood looking down at her slim fingers lying in his palm, a brooding puzzlement in his eyes. "Then you will doubly appreciate a man like Luke Storm," he said. "He is frank, above all."

"I rather pity him," Ellen commented. "He is so primitive, so governed by the impulse of the moment. So unrestrained."

"Never let Luke storm know that you pity him," Cameron warned. "He might forgive anything but that." Cameron swung to the ground. He moved ahead and overtook Luke, who was walking alongside the point yoke of oxen.

"Would you care to join me, Storm?" Cameron said, offering a cigar case filled with stogies.

Luke shook his head. *"Gracias!"* he said. "But I'll stick to my cigaritos. I picked up the habit of rollin' my smokes at Taos."

Cameron closed the case and replaced it in his pocket. He lighted his stogy from the briar pipe belonging to a Connecticut man named McDonald who was next in line. Then he freed his saddle horse from the wagon, and mounted. He waved to Ellen and Luke as he rode by, heading up the column.

Suddenly Ellen called after him. "The answer to your question, Mr. Cameron, is — is 'no'!"

Cameron twisted around. "I really had

not asked a question," he said. "And I needed no answer. I already knew."

Luke watched Cameron ride onward. Now, from the corner of an eye, he saw Ellen slowly slip from her finger the cheap wedding band that she had been wearing and drop it over the wagon side into the wheel-crushed ruts in the trail.

Luke understood. Astern of the caravan all that was visible of Independence above the brush was the weather-vane of the courthouse. That too vanished as the wagon lumbered ahead. She likely felt that she was at last beyond the reach of the law and there was no longer any need for pretense. Her role as a married woman evidently had become distasteful to her since meeting the dashing Vance Cameron. Luke had noticed how she had let her hand linger in Cameron's possession.

And he had noticed the inscription on the blue velvet lining of the cigar case Cameron had offered him. Printed in gilt was the emblem of a tobacco shop where the case had been purchased. Beneath that had been inscribed the city in which the shop was located — Baltimore, Md.

Luke was wandering if Cameron had been the mysterious intruder whom Dan Slater had surprised in his room, and who, with gunfire, had ended forever the investigator's pursuit of the dark-eyed girl.

Luke strode along beside the oxen, thinking hard. Cameron seemed to be always in the habit of turning up in Ellen Jessup's vicinity. First, on the dark street in Independence when he had seen her pass the note to Luke. Then later in the hallway at the Overland Inn after Dan Slater's murder. And now he had decided, apparently on an impulse, to join this California-bound caravan.

Tracy Menafee was now heading down the line of wagons again, returning to resume paying his respects to the pseudo Mrs. Edward Jarrett now that Vance Cameron was out of the way.

Menafee walked his horse alongside the wheel. He slung a leg over the saddlehorn and braced one arm against the rim of the wagon side while he chatted with Ellen.

Menafee was at his ease now, as he talked of the trail and its problems and his personal experiences. He had a facility with words and could be engagingly friendly.

"I'll see to it that, beginning tomorrow, your wagon will travel nearer the head of the column," Menafee said. "It is not right that you should be plagued by dust this way."

Luke spoke from his menial position with the oxen. "We'll take our turn at pilot an' in the swing an' in the dust o' the drag just as everybody else will do. We ask no favors."

Menafee was annoyed. He said to Ellen, "I had hoped our conversation was private. Apparently he takes it on himself to speak for you."

Ellen was even more annoyed. "He doesn't speak for me, naturally," she said. "But in this case I must agree with him. I will not ask any special favors. We will take our turn at the various positions in the line of march. I understand that is customary."

"As you wish." Menafee shrugged.

Al Thorne now came riding up, bringing word that the fourth wagon in Menafee's string had been repaired and would overtake the company soon. Menafee reluctantly ended his visit with Ellen and jogged away with his wagon boss.

Thorne gazed at him inquiringly. Menafee shook his head. "I learned nothing, of course. I did not expect to. I must say, however, that she is an extremely attractive lady."

"Not more attractive than two hundred thousand dollars, I hope, Tracy," Thorne murmured silkily. "And don't forget, she's a lady who helped murder her sweetheart an' dump his body in the sea."

Menafee frowned, glancing apprehensively around. "Careful, Al," he breathed. "It would be troublesome if anyone else got wind of our little secret."

"There may be at least one other person who is in on it," Thorne said. "You haven't forgotten those arrest warrants from Dan Slater's baggage that disappeared? The Missouri Kid says Slater snatched them from his hand when he surprised the Kid in his room. Who took them from Slater?"

"It couldn't have been anyone except Storm." Menafee frowned. "He was alone for seconds with Slater's body before anyone else appeared. That, I reckon, is why he was so quick to accept the job as whacker for Ellen Jessup. He's not the kind of a man to work as hired hand unless there was some purpose in it."

"That's the way I size it up also," Thorne agreed. "We've got to make sure. Storm might be carrying those papers with him. Or maybe he has them in his warsack. I'll keep an eye on him, and take a look at the warsack at first chance."

He said nothing for a moment, watching Menafee narrowly. "Once we decide for sure that he's aware of this girl's true identity I guess we know there's only one thing to do."

Again there was a silence. Menafee sat on his horse while a sickly color came into his face, and his mouth became slack and dry. He did not like to meet this question. But there was no shirking it.

This affair was like wading deeper and deeper into icy water. Each step brought its breathless repulsion. Each step also made it the more impossible to turn back — for the prize that dazzled him seemed to be just that much more attainable.

Since the previous night he and Thorne had learned considerably more about the affair in Baltimore that involved the young, dark-haired girl. They had ransacked the barbershops and taverns that morning for old copies of Eastern newspapers, and had soon found what they sought, for the establishments treasured such publications brought to Independence by the stampeders. The copies dated back for months.

They had learned that the matter had first come to light when it was discovered that Henry W. Jessup, president of the Jessup Fidelity Bank of Baltimore, and a young clerk in his establishment named Ralph Gilmore, were both mysteriously missing. An audit disclosed a shortage of roughly two hundred thousand dollars in the bank's cash.

Ralph Gilmore was a young bachelor. A search of his quarters in a modest boarding house revealed several letters whose contents were a bombshell in staid old Baltimore.

First, the authorities disclosed that they had found a letter which bore a written instruction by Gilmore that it be opened in case of his death or disappearance. The message said that if anything happened to him Henry W. Jessup should be called to account.

It appeared that Gilmore had discovered that his employer had been speculating heavily with bank funds. It placed Gilmore in a difficult position, for he was engaged to marry Jessup's daughter, Ellen, and was deeply in love with her. Because of this, Gilmore said he had agreed to say nothing, on the father's promise that the shortage in the bank's funds would be covered by a specified date. But, the letter went on, Henry Jessup in an attempt to recoup his losses had only gone deeper into default.

It was at this point that Ralph Gilmore began to fear for his life. He had discovered that his books at the bank had been tampered with in an attempt to make it appear that he was the embezzler.

The letter continued:

"I am beginning to fear that Henry Jessup is a desperate man and will stop at nothing. And I have reason to know that Ellen is aware of her father's predicament and is desperately afraid of the disgrace exposure will bring to her."

All of this evidently had been a tremendous sensation in Baltimore where Henry W. Jessup, who was a widower and a descendant of an aristocratic family, had been regarded as a man of impeccable integrity.

Then had come the second sensation. The authorities had revealed that another letter had been found in Ralph Gilmore's room, addressed to Miss Ellen Jessup, and evidently intended for mailing.

This letter was apparently an answer to a long and tense private talk Gilmore and Ellen had had a few days previously. The import was that Ellen had come to Gilmore to plead with him to take the blame for the embezzlement by fleeing from Baltimore. She had promised that she would join him and live with him, either with or without the benefit of marriage, as a reward for this sacrifice. Ellen had even proposed that Gilmore help himself liberally to whatever cash in the bank he could lay hands on before fleeing.

Gilmore's letter was a sad and shocked refusal of this proposal. He forgave Ellen on the grounds that the strain of her father's predicament had caused her to lose her sense of moral values. He made it plain that he was washing his hands of the whole affair.

Ralph Gilmore had never got around to mailing this letter. It was found in a stamped envelope in the pocket of a smoking jacket in his room.

He had left his quarters suddenly the same evening, dressed in his best. A note in Ellen Jessup's handwriting had been found on the bureau, inviting him to the Jessup residence for a late supper. Gilmore had left in a rented carriage. The driver testified under oath later that he had delivered his fare at the gate of the Jessup mansion on the outskirts of the city about nine o'clock of that misty, cool evening in June.

That was the last time Ralph Gilmore was ever seen alive. And Henry Jessup also had vanished mysteriously the same night.

Ellen Jessup had denied everything, including Gilmore's written statement that she had offered to sell herself to protect her father. She had denied that she had written the note inviting Gilmore to her home, and denied that they had been engaged to be married. But nobody believed her. She was tried and convicted both in the newspapers and in public opinion.

Exhaustive questioning by the authorities had failed to break her down. She claimed that on the night Gilmore and her father had disappeared she had been in her bedroom reading while her father worked on business matters in his study downstairs. She claimed she had not discovered that he was missing until morning.

Ellen Jessup was in an ugly position. It seemed obvious that Ralph Gilmore had met with foul play and that she had lured him into a trap. This was borne out by reports from two witnesses who were positive they had seen her father in a curtained carriage, driving at a gallop down a back road out of Baltimore late on the night of the disappearances. But there was no tangible evidence on which to arrest her.

Then nearly a month later, when the sensation was beginning to die in public interest, a fish-eaten, decomposed body that was identified by a ring and scraps of clothing as that of Ralph Gilmore, was found floating in Chesapeake Bay.

The skull had been crushed with a blow from some heavy weapon. At last evidence of murder had been found. Police rushed to arrest Ellen Jessup, who had moved to a modest room in a middle-class district in Baltimore, for the Jessup mansion had been seized by the court to help satisfy the bank shortage. But Ellen Jessup was gone. She had fled Baltimore just ahead of the authorities.

Menafee sat on his horse, thinking of all this while he weighed his response to Al Thorne's statement. For it had been a statement rather than a question. ". . . I guess we know there's only one thing to do," Thorne had said.

Menafee took his time. Now that he had the full details of the crime he was more certain than ever that Ellen was heading for California to meet her father at some previously appointed place. And there was reason to suppose that the greater part of the two hundred thousand embezzled dollars was still in Henry Jessup's possession.

For Ralph Gilmore evidently had been wrong in assuming that Henry Jessup had squandered his peculations away in stock gambling. According to the newspaper accounts no evidence of such operations had been uncovered, nor of any other extravagant expenditures by the banker. Henry Jessup had fled with the cash intact.

Menafee drew a long, reluctant breath. "Yes," he murmured finally. "You will know what to do, Al."

The arid glint of a smile flickered across Al Thorne's sparse lips. "*We* will know what to do," he corrected Menafee. "We are in this together, Tracy. We split everything even — the work as well as the money."

"Yes," Menafee said, his voice uncertain. "Yes, Al."

Thus was another murder pledged — the murder of Luke Storm or anyone else who might endanger their own hopes.

Chapter VII

The wagons nooned briefly, then moved on again through the blazing heat of the afternoon. Luke walked beside the oxen, his wide-brimmed hat pulled low to shade his eyes from the glare. He unlaced the buckskin shirt and finally removed it entirely and hovered in the shadow of the wagon whenever possible for the sake of coolness. He had tied a scarf of finest silk over the lower part of his face, for at times the boil of dust from the wheels and hooves came upon him in a suffocating cloud.

They had emerged temporarily from the timber and brush into a sun-baked open stretch where the soil was sandy and barren. Here the heat of the day generated whirling dust devils which sprang into life erratically and vanished just as quickly. The beginnings of thunderheads loomed in the sky above timbered hills ahead. Luke could see men and women along the line gazing at those distant purple hills, a sudden uncertainty in their expressions.

This, he knew, was the moment when the crushing realization of parting with the past bore down upon them. This was the time when they wanted to hide from this challenge — to turn back to their own kind. But, for him, it was going home.

A child began to wail in one of the wagons ahead. That would be six-year-old Honey Downs. Luke had seen Ellen try to make friends with the little, tow-headed girl during the nooning stop. But Honey had been quickly snatched away by her mother.

Jenny Downs had made it plain she did not want her child to come in contact with the notorious Mrs. Edward Jarrett. There were half a dozen other women in the company and Luke had seen their condemning expressions. They shared Jenny Downs' opinion. Ellen was branded as a loose and dissolute woman and the members of her sex meant to pillory her during this long journey. Grimly Luke visualized their consternation if they were to learn that the pseudo Mrs. Jarrett was also wanted for murder.

The gusty wind seemed to have subsided. Ellen gathered her skirts about her legs and descended from the slow-moving wagon. The dust and heat beneath the hood, and the jostling had become intolerable.

She opened a small parasol as a protection from the sun. "I believe I'll walk for a while," she told Luke lightly. "I need the exercise."

"A right smart idea," Luke nodded. "An' it'd be better if your gentlemen callers stayed off the wagon too. Every ounce the cattle can avoid pullin' now will help 'em just that much a couple o' months from now on the Humboldt Desert an' in Carson Sink, when they'll need their strength."

Ellen bridled and the parasol bobbed indignantly. "I'm sure Mr. Cameron's short visit placed no strain on the oxen," she said. "My wagon carries the lightest load in the company. There's nothing but my pallet and trunk and the stock of food."

"It won't always be that way, you hear me now," Luke said. "There'll be dead oxen an' busted wagons an' doublin' up needed before this pasear is finished. The most of these wagons are overloaded. Like the preacher's. He's only got three yoke o' oxen an' he's packin' all his family furniture. He aims to carry his manner of livin' all the way to the Sandwich Islands. He'll have to start shuckin' that foofaraw before he reaches the first Platte ford. An' he won't be the only one."

"Perhaps you think I should walk all the way to California," Ellen said stiffly.

He eyed her appraisingly. "It'd be best for you at that," he added. "Sittin' in that wagon for two thousand miles would sure broaden you in places other than your viewpoint. Like Mike McDuffy's wife there ahead. Maggie McDuffy'll soon be an ax handle acrost. She's already rode all the way from Ohio."

Ellen tried to glare him down. That was a mistake, for Luke only gave her a devilish leer. In addition, she was at an increasing disadvantage, for the wind was springing up again and her wide skirt and many petticoats were a distinct liability. Also she was realizing that slippers were not the sort of thing for this type of going.

To add to her tribulations at that instant one of the whirlies soared into violent life and swooped down upon them. The parasol was whipped from Ellen's hand. She found herself desperately battling to hold down her skirts — with only indifferent success. She was twirled around dizzily and would have fallen, had not Luke reached her side in time to steady her.

The whirlie passed. The oxen, which had halted momentarily, resumed their stoic pace. Luke chased the parasol across the sand hummocks, retrieved it and returned it to her considerably the worse for wear.

Ellen tried to restore her dignity. "I seem to have made a spectacle of myself," she said.

"Yep," Luke agreed. "It was quite a sight. But you got nothing to be ashamed of. Fact is the only damage done was to make these other womenfolk madder'n ever at you. You got the right kind of a shape for windy days. They'll hold that against you above everything else."

"You make yourself offensive with your impudent vulgarity," Ellen exploded. "I'm sure you'll be happier elsewhere. I'll pay you a week's wages tonight and hire another driver."

Luke looked at her steadily and said, "You've got the wrong attitude on this trip. Also the wrong kind of clothes. Britches an' good stout shoes and sunbonnets are what you'll find the handiest. We'll likely pass a trader along the way who can fix you up. You can pack away all them ruffles an' buttons you got on until you hit Hangtown."

Ellen stamped her foot. "Don't you understand that I'm discharging you?" she exclaimed.

"I don't need your protection," Luke said. "Nor that fancy-dressed Cameron's either."

"You — you heard what Mr. Cameron and I were saying?" she demanded indignantly.

"Hell's purple flames!" Luke snorted. "How could I help it? I wasn't twenty feet away!"

"Well . . . well . . . !" Ellen said helplessly.

She was defeated. She fled precipitantly. She scrambled aboard the wagon and over the bow and dropped into the security of the interior.

Luke Storm, she reflected, was intolerable. Yet he was a man for his environment, she conceded. Every move he made, everything he wore or owned was exactly right for its purpose. Other men were making hard going of it over the heat-drenched hummocks and wheel ruts and loose sand, but Luke moved along in his soft, noiseless moccasins without apparent effort, his long legs lazily matching the patient gait of the oxen.

In fact he appeared to be almost asleep on his feet. Evidently he had the faculty of complete relaxation, no matter what the discomfort or the circumstances. Like an animal, she reflected. And also, like an animal, his hearing evidently was far more acute than the humans with whom she was accustomed to associating. Otherwise he could not have overheard her conversation with Vance Cameron above the creak and rumble of the wagons and the scuffle of plodding hooves.

She bitterly regretted the turn of chance that had brought him across her path. She had the sensation of total entanglement — of being swept along by forces she could not resist nor control, forces that were as elemental and unchangeable as Luke Storm's nature appeared to be.

On the other hand, she was on her way to an unknown land. She was an outcast among her own sex for the duration of the journey at least, and only because she had intervened to save this overbearing mountain man from the same fate that hovered over her — the noose. She was utterly alone, completely cut off from the world she had known. It came to her, startlingly, that she was, in fact, almost entirely dependent now upon Luke Storm.

She was aroused by a girl's voice outside the wagon calling, "Mrs. Jarrett! Mrs. Jarrett!"

Ellen peered out. Abbie Wallace was alongside. "May I come aboard?" Abbie asked, smiling. "That's a seagoing expression, I know, but it seems appropriate out here. I would very much like to become acquainted with you, Mrs. Jarrett."

"Why — why — !" Ellen said. "Of course!"

Surprisingly, Luke halted the oxen and helped the lithe, chestnut-haired missionary girl over the wheel and up the step into the wagon.

Ellen saw Jenny Downs' and Mrs. McDuffy's and other sunbonneted heads turned all along the line, faces staring with shocked disapproval.

Abbie Wallace pointedly ignored them. In the hot interior of the wagon she smoothed her calico dress, kicked off her shoes and looked at Ellen with a frank and friendly smile. "If I'm intruding I hope you will tell me," she said. "But as you and I are of about the same age I wanted to make friends. I brought along my knitting."

"But are you sure you want to do this, my dear?" Ellen asked. "Your uncle will disapprove. And the other ladies are scandalized. I imagine you know that I am supposed to be a soiled dove."

Abbie said calmly, "Bosh! They're only a

flock of hens scratching in the dirt." She looked Ellen over and smiled. "I do not believe you are either a dove or soiled. You look like a girl with too much spunk to be called a dove, and, as for being soiled, I imagine a female as attractive as you are could do considerably better than a drunken mountain man like Luke Storm if she were in the mood for romance."

Ellen laughed suddenly. It struck her that this was the first time she had laughed with real enjoyment since that nightmare had first come upon her at Baltimore.

"Thank you," she said. "Thank you, Miss Wallace."

"My name is Abigail," the missionary girl said. "Abbie to my friends. And yours is . . . ?"

"Ellen," she said. She regretted it the instant she had spoken. She had meant to use a pseudonym, but Abbie Wallace's friendliness had struck a warm responsive chord within her. Suddenly she had wanted, in this one instance at least, to be truthful.

But evidently the similarity between her assumed name of Ellen Jarrett and the real one of Ellen Jessup meant nothing to Abbie Wallace. Ellen breathed easily again.

She seated Abbie on the pallet, opened

the bow curtains and, rolled the side sheets to admit more air. "I'm sorry to admit it, but I neglected to bring my own knitting bag," she said. "But if what Luke Storm says is true, there'll be little time for knitting. He seems to think we are in for a hard journey. But I'm sure he is only trying to frighten us. He wants to impress me with his own importance, and —"

Her voice drifted off into a panicky halt. She had remembered Luke's acute sense of hearing. She rose and peered out fearfully. To her relief Luke was with the point yoke, moving along with a half-asleep stride that expended a minimum of energy.

Then Luke turned and eyed her witheringly. "You better learn to keep your voices down before we get into Indian country, or you'll have every squaw from the forks of the Platte to the Digger country laughin' at me," he snorted.

Ellen sank back, crushed. "That — that barbarian!" she murmured. "He hears everything a person says, knows everything I even think. He's even trying to tell me how to dress, and that I ought to do more walking to — to reduce my — my hips."

"Somebody had to tell you," Luke observed without turning his head.

After that the girls dropped their voices to

a cautious whisper. Luke grinned. He rolled one of his brown-paper cigaritos and borrowed a light from Andy McDonald's pipe. For the moment, at least, he was content.

The caravan reached a stream late in the afternoon. The watercourse was relatively insignificant to Luke, but the majority of the company stared uneasily. In the orderly pattern of the settled lands from which they had come they had never thought of a stream without also thinking of a bridge. Now they were confronted by the first reality of the journey.

This creek was only a few rods in width and below wagon bed depth at the deepest but the banks were brushy and steep where a new approach to the stream had been hacked through the willows and alder. It was evident that once a heavy wagon was committed to the descent through the brush there would be no holding back. And the stream bed, Luke reported after an inspection, was soft and might turn quicksandy with use.

"Maybe we better camp here for the night," the husband of Carrie Philips said uneasily. "We can ford in the morning when the stock is better rested."

Others began to nod quick agreement.

"Camp?" Luke protested. "Why, it's still an hour to sundown an' we'll have another hour or more of twilight after that to pitch camp. We can do three, four more miles before we outspan. You, there in the wagons ahead, keep rollin'. That ford is easy if you handle your teams."

"Are you advising us to make a dry camp farther on?" the father of Honey Downs objected uncertainly.

"A dry camp won't do any harm," Luke said. "The stock can water here as they ford. Tonight they'll have good grass with dew on it to feed on. We'll hit next water at noonin' time tomorrow. We'll be miles ahead instead of losin' valuable time here."

Tracy Menafee came riding up, belatedly exuding the authority of captain. "What's the delay?" he demanded. "We're wasting time. Storm, are you advising these men to camp here tonight? Ridiculous! We must take advantage of every hour, every minute if these people are to reach California this year. We must push on at once."

Vance Cameron, who had joined the group, murmured in Luke's ear. "The devil a saint will be. He seems to be trying to make you out as a false prophet, Storm."

Luke was puzzled. If that was Menafee's purpose then he had scored his point.

Chapter VIII

Disgruntled, Luke walked to Ellen's wagon. "I'll lead the way across this mud puddle," he said.

He picked up the goad and spoke to the oxen. "Hi — y — ! Hike!"

The cattle bowed their necks and lifted the lightly laden wagon out of its tracks. Ellen stared apprehensively at the descent to the stream. Suddenly she scrambled over the side and dropped to the ground. She had no faith in Luke either.

Luke drove past the waiting wagons. "If'n the rest o' you aim to be scared," he said derisively, "save it for the first Platte crossing. But right now, mind how I handle this crick an' do the same. Once you start down the slant keep them cattle stretched out on the chain. Don't let the wagon push 'em. Use the brake. Some of the heavier ones better be chain-locked. There's a two-foot drop-off when you hit the water an' if your wheels ain't in control they'll cramp an' maybe capsize you."

The popper on his whip exploded. "Hi-yah!" he yelled.

The oxen broke into a lumbering trot and the wagon tilted down the slant. Oxen and wagon hit the stream with a splash. The team lurched through the belly-deep water like beavers, prodded faster by the sound of the whip and Luke's voice.

Luke, wading to his waist, grinned back at Ellen who was standing with Abbie, watching. With all the oxen pulling smoothly, he snaked the wagon across the stream and up the opposite ascent to level ground beyond the ford.

Then he returned to the stream to help the others. He waded back and forth with the churning wagons, his urgent voice barking impatient directions. Vance Cameron, on his black horse, was also in the stream helping to keep the wagons moving. "Storm!" Cameron finally whirled on Luke in exasperation. "Don't yell at us like children. I resent —"

He broke off. The wagon owned by the father of little Honey Downs had just started down the slant to the ford. The child and her mother were huddled together apprehensively on a seat that had been built across the bow. Honey Downs had a doll in her arms, and was clinging to the forward bow with one small hand.

Her father was shouting nervously at the oxen, and his uncertainty had communicated itself to the animals. George Downs had been a bookkeeper in a small Indiana town who had come into a small inheritance. He had, on an impulse, decided to attempt this journey with his young wife and small child in the hope of making a real fortune in the gold mines. But he had no experience at handling oxen and a heavy wagon. George Downs was out of his element, and frightened. And now the wagon and team were getting out of control.

Luke and Cameron saw the trouble coming. Cameron whirled his horse and spurred through the mud-churned water. Luke caught a stirrup and ran with long, splashing strides.

George Downs' wagon was snaking from side to side. The cattle, suddenly going into a panic, tried to balk. The wagon overran them, shoving the animals ahead. The oxen at once swerved off the trail, crashing into the willow thickets. That cramped the wheels. The wagon veered sharply, and that abrupt movement sent little Honey Downs toppling from the seat. Her mother snatched at her and missed.

The child screamed as she pitched headlong to the ground. She landed directly in the path of the oncoming left front wheel. She would have been crushed at once, but, by a stroke of fortune, a heavy tree root stood exposed above the earth here, and her small body landed in its downslope shelter.

The wheel halted momentarily as it reached this obstruction. It paused there, looming over the stunned child's body as the weight of the wagon cramped the running gear in the opposite direction. Once this movement had reached its limit, the wheel would be driven forward over the tree root to drop upon the small girl and crush her to death.

Luke was first to arrive, for Cameron's horse had been impeded by the brush. He dived among the plunging oxen and snatched at the child's limp form. But Honey Downs' calico skirt was firmly caught by the wheel. Before Luke could shift balance and rip the dress free he felt the weight of the wagon coming down on his shoulder. The child was almost directly beneath him.

He stood braced, attempting to halt the

weight that bore down impersonally upon them. Then Cameron reached his side and also wedged himself beneath the juggernaut that would mangle both them and the child in moments.

Luke saw the veins stand out in Cameron's face. Men were shouting and women were screaming, but these sounds were vague above the roaring in Luke's ears as he strained against the burden that was inexorably descending upon them.

Then two feminine figures entered the danger zone in the wagon's path. Ellen and Abbie. Luke tried to order them away, but found he had no voice.

Ellen seized the knife from his belt and slashed away the fold of calico that held Honey Downs trapped, while Abbie dragged the child out of danger.

The wheel descended on the spot where Honey Downs had lain. Neither Luke nor Cameron had the strength to escape from its path. Their muscles were paralyzed. They would be crushed. Then Abbie seized Cameron and yanked him clear. At the same instant Ellen caught Luke by his shoulders and hurled herself backward, bringing him with her by her own weight.

The wagon lurched wildly and seemed about to capsize upon them. Then it righted itself and lunged onward down the descent, finally crashing into the brush and bringing up against a sycamore at the margin of the stream.

Luke got shakily to his knees. His lungs still wheezed agonizingly. He had the taste of blood in his throat. Ellen was sitting alongside him, but too spent to make any further effort at the moment. Cameron pulled himself to his knees, then staggered to his feet. He too was wheezing like a man who had been shot through the lungs. Abbie stood with little Honey Downs in her arms. Honey now began to weep in terror.

Luke lifted Ellen to her feet. "Don't you know any better'n to crawl under a wagon that's runnin' loose?" he fumed. He glared at Abbie and Cameron. "That goes for all o' you," he raged. You might have been squashed like tumblebugs! Blast it, don't ever do anything like that again!"

He turned upon the other wagon people. "Quit standin' there like a flock o' geese an' get the wagons movin'," he barked. "We've lost enough time already with this foolishness."

Cameron and the girls looked at each other, astounded. "You ungrateful person!" Abbie blazed at Luke. "You ought to thank

Mrs. Jarrett and Mr. Cameron from the bottom of your heart, instead of shouting at them. You —"

Ellen touched her arm, halting her. "Never mind, Abbie," she said. "It doesn't matter. It's his pride that's hurt because mere greenhorns had to come to his help. What really matters is that Honey Downs is safe."

Luke saw Menafee and Al Thorne in the background, with the other members of their crew who had left their wagons to run to the scene of the excitement. None had turned a hand to help. The faces of Menafee and Thorne were blank, without emotion. But Mack Sledge and Missouri Kid were palpably disappointed that Luke had emerged unscathed.

"A brave deed, Storm," Menafee said in a loud, praising voice. "You deserve reward. I'll take up a collection for you tonight in camp and start it with a gold piece of my own."

"Sure," Luke said evenly, "an' I'll ram every coin right down the throat of the man that gives it — includin' your own, Tracy."

Menafee turned to the others, spreading his hands in a gesture of helpless shock. "A violent, strange man," he said.

Luke, his voice sharp and intolerant, prodded the wagon people into action. The Downs wagon was double-teamed out of its position, and moved across the stream. It had sustained only minor damage that could be taken care of later.

Luke seethed inwardly. Ellen had told the truth. It hurt his pride and shook his sense of self-sufficiency to have to admit that two young females and a soft-voiced greenhorn had saved him. Worse yet, he was now deeper in debt to Ellen Jessup. And he was now indebted almost equally to Vance Cameron. And to Abbie Wallace also, though there was less injury to his self-esteem in this respect, for he felt that he understood the impulsive, warm-eyed missionary girl. There would be no aura of obligation or debt over anything Abbie did for him or any other member of this wagon train, for it was her nature and her training to be loyal to a comradeship and to expect loyalty and sacrifice.

But he did not understand Ellen Jessup. Why would a person accused of being a party to brutal murder face the risk of mangling and agonizing death to save someone else? Luke watched Cameron riding alongside the wagon, chatting with the two girls. Both Ellen and Abbie seemed to have taken their brush with death calmly enough. Luke had to confess that he held a grudging respect for the three of them. Evidently they were of more durable fiber than he had given them credit for.

The caravan camped when the long twilight began to deepen. Luke outspanned the oxen from Ellen's wagon and turned the animals into the stock herd. Tracy Menafee called the men together and counted off the crews who would stand stock guard in shifts. Menafee was acting as captain, and apparently intended to remain in that capacity during the entire trip.

As Luke turned away he collided with the massive, grizzly-like Mack Sledge. Sledge shouldered him roughly. Luke gave Sledge his arid grin and left him standing there. In the background he saw the crooked face of the Missouri Kid watching from the shadows.

So this was the way it shaped up. Luke could understand the grudges that Sledge and the Missouri Kid held against him and could expect any type of violent retaliation from them. He had also offended Tracy Menafee and Al Thorne and they likely would welcome any bad luck that befell him. Still . . . in the eyes of Thorne and Menafee he had seen something deeper and more irrevocable. It was as though their intentions toward him went beyond mere personal affairs.

Uneasily he carried this thought with him as he gathered fuel for the supper fire and hurried to the stock herd to help locate the animals on graze. Full darkness had come, and the sky was a-glitter with stars before he headed back to the wagon circle. Cook fires were glowing and the fragrance of food and coffee reminded him that he was very hungry. He began hurrying, thinking of the meal that Ellen should have ready by this time.

He pulled up, staring outraged, as he reached the wagon. A great fire, the biggest in camp, was burning furiously, and Ellen, driven back by its heat, hovered anxiously on its fringe.

She had unloaded food boxes and utensils from the wagon. A sack of flour had been opened and upset so that some of its contents had spilled into the dust. A side of smoked meat was unwrapped and someone had hacked off a few very ragged slices with a kitchen knife before giving up the attempt. Dutch ovens, skillets and the coffee pot stood about — ready but empty.

Luke gazed disbelievingly at the leaping fire. Evidently Ellen had heaped the entire supply of fuel on the conflagration. "Hell's whiskers!" he exploded. "You can't even cook! Why you got a fire there big enough to roast an ox, along with the yoke."

Ellen spoke between set lips. "I'm sorry. I'll learn. I'll do better."

"An' what'll I do while you're learnin'?" Luke demanded. "Starve?"

"You can starve or you can go to — to perdition for all I care!" she exclaimed, her eyes glistening with humiliation.

Luke got a pail of water from the wagon barrel and reduced the fire. Presently he had the small bed of hot coals that he wanted. He soon had biscuits in the dutch oven and coffee heating. He got a skillet of potatoes and onions frying. With his belt knife he sliced smoked meat neatly.

Ellen stood by, humiliated and smoldering, but too proud to retreat to the refuge of the wagon. When the meal was ready he filled a plate and passed it to her.

"That'll have to do for a quick bait," he said. "Time we hit buffalo country, it'll be different." His voice grew ecstatic. "Buffalo! Wait'll you sink your teeth in hump ribs from a young cow. Roasted slow an' drippin' brown. Or fleece stewed with such greens as a person can find. Or boudins."

"Boudins?" Ellen asked. "What are they?"

"Guts," Luke said casually. "Fine eatin'. Add a touch o' gall. Keeps away scurvy."

Ellen, in spite of her anger, had been unable to resist Luke's cooking. She had started to eat with a keen appetite. Now he saw her go a trifle pale around the lips. She started to lay the plate aside. Then she saw his ironic eyes watching her. She stiffened. By sheer force of will she overcame her squeamishness. Grimly she tackled the food again.

Luke thoughtfully turned to the boiling coffee pot. It was becoming more and more evident that there was no real frailty beneath Ellen Jessup's beauty and refinement. She seemed equal to any occasion, evidently. . . . Even to murder, Luke reflected, and he was aware of a hideous sense of unreality.

At that moment somewhat of a procession came into their fire circle. Abbie Wallace, carrying an armload of clothing, led the way. She was accompanied by her Aunt Martha, a small, neatly dressed woman. Towering at their heels was the gangling forbidding figure of her uncle and George Downs. Between them they were carrying a bulky, canvas-covered object of unwieldy shape.

Luke put down the coffee pot and got to his feet, staring. Ellen spoke. "I have asked Miss Wallace to move in with me, Mr. Storm. Her uncle's wagon is heavily loaded and I have plenty of room."

She expected reprimand. Instead Luke nodded approvingly. "You're learning," he said. "Now, maybe the preacher's wagon will last a couple weeks longer than I figured before we have to take on some more of his load."

Chapter IX

The Rev. Emery Dixon and his companion set their burden down. Luke now identified it by its shape as the harp that Abbie had been playing at the celebration in Independence.

The minister said stiffly, "I still trust that you will reconsider, Abigail." It was plain from his demeanor that this was the climax of a long family struggle that he had lost.

"Uncle, dear!" Abbie protested, "I'm not leaving you. I'll always be within call."

"On my knees I will try to justify myself to your dead father and mother for permitting this," Emery Dixon said sadly. "Come, Martha! There is nothing more to say."

He took his wife's arm and led her away. He had ignored Luke and Ellen entirely.

George Downs stood shifting from one foot to another. "Mr. Storm," he burst out, "I want you to know that me and Jenny are mighty grateful for what you did to save

Honey at the ford today. And you too, Mrs. Jarrett. And Miss Abigail."

It was Abbie who spoke. "Tell Mrs. Downs it might be better if she thanked Mrs. Jarrett personally."

"I sure will," the man promised and beat a hasty retreat from a situation that was embarrassing him.

Ellen gazed at Abbie. "Please!" she said tiredly. "It doesn't matter."

"But it does!" Abbie exclaimed. "What right have they to condemn you?"

Ellen smiled wanly. "The real reason you are moving in with me is to try to make them admit they are wrong," she said. "To protect me. That is it, isn't it, Abbie dearest?"

"Missionary work," Abbie said, "is not always exclusively for the benefit of the heathen sea islanders. It seems there is a rich field right here in this caravan."

"Why are you so — so sure of me?" Ellen asked.

Luke spoke roughly. "She already told you why this afternoon. She told you a lady like you would never a' had anything to do with a drunken mountain man."

The two girls looked at him.

Luke hadn't intended to give them this glimpse of the resentment that had been gnawing at him. He changed the subject swiftly, glaring at the canvas-shielded harp. "You don't aim to pack that thing all the way to California?" he demanded.

It was Ellen who answered. "And why not?"

Luke ran his fingers wildly through his tawny hair. "Why not, she asks," he moaned. "Don't she know that it's better to put the weight in grain for the cattle? All a harp is good for on a trip like this is to send us to heaven."

At this point the coffee pot boiled over. In rescuing it Luke burned a finger, and that brought forth a vigorous "Damnation!"

"It is very evident that your own chances of reaching heaven need improving," Abbie said severely. "I will pray for you, Luke Storm."

"Could I be included in the prayer?" Vance Cameron inquired, strolling into the firelight. Luke surmised that he had been standing in the background for some time, listening.

Abbie stiffened. "You probably would benefit," she said neutrally. "I am told that you gamble with cards and drink."

"Guilty," Cameron said. "If they are sins, then I am a sinner."

Cameron lighted one of his stogies and stood puffing and at ease while Abbie and Ellen busied themselves at the dishpan. Luke noticed that he now carried his supply of smokes in the breast pocket of his shirt.

Cameron and Ellen continued their bantering small talk. Luke saw that, for the moment, a new Ellen Jessup had come to the surface. Animation was in her eyes and voice. It was as though she were eagerly grasping at some part of her life that was lost.

Luke finished his coffee, left out of the talk. He was sitting with them, but was a world apart from them and their thoughts and interests. He was still alone, as he had been ever since his parents had gone away during that terrible winter when he was a boy.

He rose and went to the wagon. He and Cameron would be on duty later with the second watch on stock guard. He saw by the stars that they still had thirty minutes or more before reporting.

He lifted his bedroll and possible sack out of Ellen's wagon. Heavy clouds in the sky to the west might bring rain before morning, so he spread the tarp and laid out his blankets beneath the vehicle for the sake of shelter. He unlaced the drawstring on his possible sack, and got out what items he would need in the morning. Emerging from beneath the wagon, he paused to listen.

At the opposite side of the fire Ellen was saying, "I'm a Marylander by birth. I was born and lived as a child in Baltimore. Are you acquainted in Baltimore, Mr. Cameron?"

"Unfortunately not, Mrs. Jarrett," Cameron said. "I've only passed through by train. I'm a hidebound New Yorker."

Luke listened tensely, but the conversation drifted away into other channels. He knew Ellen had brought up the name of her home city for a purpose. He wondered if that meant that she was suspicious of Vance Cameron. He doubted that. More likely, he reasoned, she was merely taking the precaution to make sure Cameron was not familiar with the city where she was wanted by the law.

He wondered what had happened to the cigar case from Baltimore which Cameron no longer carried, and of the easy denial that he had ever been in that city.

Luke stood up, rolled himself a cigarito and wandered off into the darkness in the direction of the stock herd.

Ellen suddenly fell silent. Cameron looked at her inquiringly.

"I tried to discharge him," Ellen explained defensively, "but he had overheard our talk. I bruised my authority against his pride. It was like striking flint. He is an uncouth, stubborn man."

"Stubborn perhaps," Cameron said. "But not as uncouth as he would have us believe."

"What do you mean?"

"I learned a few things about Luke Storm today from an old plainsman named Eli Brass who came by, heading for Independence. He told me that Luke Storm's father was an ordained minister of the Gospel."

Abbie aroused. "A minister?" she exclaimed. Her eyes widened. "Not Martin Storm? I've heard of him. Surely you don't mean . . . ?"

Cameron nodded. "Like your own uncle, Luke's father was a missionary. He was famed as an orator. Luke's mother was also a highly educated person, according to Brass. Luke accompanied them west when he was still a boy. They were bound for Oregon with a party of immigrants to preach to the tribes of the Northwest. But their party was overtaken by winter in the Shoshone country on the Snake River."

Ellen and Abbie were standing frozen. Abbie's hands were clasped tightly together as though in prayer. She knew the story of Martin Storm.

"Luke's mother became ill," Cameron went on. "The other members of the company deserted them, leaving Luke and his parents to make out as best they could. Luke's father and mother died of starvation. He was at the point of death also when he was found by a party of trappers. They took him with them and he became a mountain man. But he had already received Christian training and considerable education. Apparently he has added to this by self-teaching. You may have noticed that he occasionally abandons the mountain way of talking and uses the language of an educated person. The other, I am sure, is only an affectation with him."

"I've noticed," Ellen agreed. "That must explain why he holds wagon people in such low regard."

"And missionaries like me in particular," Abbie said. "He thinks we also would desert him to save ourselves."

"Who knows what we would do if we were put to a hard decision like that?" Ellen said slowly. "He may be right."

Cameron nodded. "Seeing his own mother and father starve isn't exactly the kind of an experience to cause him to be charitable or trusting toward humanity."

The call for the second night guard to report for duty sounded. "That means me," Cameron said. He picked up his slicker and rifle and said good night. He strode off to overtake Luke.

A moment later Ellen saw the shadow of a massive man detach itself from the bulk of a wagon in the background. It was the heavy-shouldered Mack Sledge. He went shuffling off into the blackness. A dread moved through her. She surmised that Sledge must have been lurking there for some time, watching their party — watching Luke Storm.

"I'm going to warn Storm about that awful man," she said suddenly. And she hurried off in the direction Cameron and Luke had gone.

The remainder of the camp was settling down for the night. Abbie was thinking of what she had learned about Luke's background. With a woman's curiosity she peered beneath the wagon at the bed he had made. She was a little piqued to find it neatly in order, with the blankets precisely arranged. Not even a woman could have done better, she had to admit. He had laid out his razor and strop and brush on the wagon perch for quick action in the morning, along with a clean blue cotton shirt, socks and underwear. She realized that, contrary to first impression, Luke Storm was an extremely fastidious man.

His possible sack was hung over the perch also, and the drawstring had not been relaced. Abbie saw the shape of what was undoubtedly a book outlined against the canvas material. Her curiosity was too keen to be denied. She had to know what type of reading material this man would carry on his travels in view of his criticism of other persons who burdened the oxen with items that he regarded as useless weight.

She glanced around guiltily to make sure nobody was watching. Silencing her conscience at this brazen breach of privacy, she crawled beneath the wagon, seated herself on the blankets and thrust an arm into the bag.

She drew out the book. It was a Bible which had been rebound in tough buffalo leather. She turned to a flyleaf. It bore an inscription in a woman's small, rounded penmanship. She held the page to catch the glow of the campfire, and read:

>   Independence,
>   July 31, 1836
> To our beloved son, Luke, on the joyful occasion of his fourteenth birthday. May God's message always accompany him and be forever in his heart.
>   His Loving Mother and Father

Tears flowed down Abbie's cheeks. So that fatal journey that had cost Luke's parents their lives had started in midsummer also — and from the same point as this present company had set forth. No wonder, she reflected, that he had been so grim and insistent in warning them of the risk.

She started to replace the Bible in the bag. But some papers that had been concealed between the pages fell fluttering into her lap. She picked them up, intending to return them to their hiding place. Then she paused, staring at the bold black print across the top of one of the dog-eared items:

WANTED FOR MURDER!

Now she saw that the other two papers were legal documents. Warrants for the arrest of persons named Ellen Marie Jessup and Henry W. Jessup. Automatically she read the small type on the reward poster. Her eyes, stunned, traveled again over the printed description of Ellen Marie Jessup.

"Ellen!" She almost screamed in horror. Suddenly she thrust the papers back inside the Bible and jammed the Book into its place in Luke's bag.

She scuttled from beneath the wagon as though pursued by Satan. As she rose to her feet, a man crouching in the darkness beyond the wagon swung an arm and hurled a silent, evil object. The heavy knife blade caught the glint of the firelight in its flight.

It struck Abbie in the back. The force of it drove her staggering forward on her knees. She clung to a wagon wheel while agony raced through her, hot and savage. It was many moments before she could find the strength to cry out.

By that time Al Thorne had faded away into the shadows. Ever since camp had been made, he had been waiting for an opportunity to search Luke's belongings. Abbie had saved him the trouble, for there could be no question as to the identity of the papers he had seen her reading.

It also removed any doubt that Luke Storm knew the secret of Ellen Jessup's past. Abbie had stumbled upon that knowledge also, and it had become necessary to put her out of the way, just as Luke must be removed. Thorne had taken advantage of opportunity and had acted swiftly and mercilessly. He reasoned that the missionary girl would have immediately exposed Ellen Jessup to the entire company as a fugitive. That would have ended any hope that the plum he and Menafee were playing for would ever fall into their possession.

Thorne was at some distance when the shouting and excitement began around Ellen's wagon. Presently he saw Luke and Ellen come racing into the firelight, followed by Vance Cameron.

Luke pushed through the wagon people who were gathering about Abbie. She still clung dazedly to the wheel, her body slumped against the spokes. Luke saw the knife jutting from her back.

"Oh . . . oh!" Ellen gasped in a fading voice.

Luke shook her roughly. "This is no time to faint!" he snapped. "You're needed!"

He brought out his knife and slit the back of Abbie's calico waist, exposing the area where the blade had entered her flesh.

"Anybody in this outfit know anything

about doctoring?" he asked, looking around.

Emery Dixon, his nightshirt stuffed into hastily donned breeches, pushed Luke aside, knelt beside his niece and peered close at the wound. He gently tested the knife. His bony, big-knuckled hands had sureness and authority.

Finally he looked up. "Fix a pallet by the fire and feed on more wood for quick light," he commanded. "I'll need laudanum, bandages and warm water. And possibly a keen knife or two. And good linen thread and a needle."

"The blade seems to have glanced off the shoulder blade," Luke said. "It evidently has missed the lung."

"That is my hope," Emery Dixon murmured. "An ugly wound, but not necessarily fatal, provided the poor child can withstand the shock of what I must do."

Luke bent close and examined the knife that Emery Dixon was making preparations to remove. It was a commonplace skinning knife of a make that was sold by the hundreds on the frontier. There was no way of telling who had owned it.

Emery Dixon administered the opiate, and when it took effect he removed the knife slowly, carefully. It was evident that this was not the first time he had been called upon to doctor the flesh as well as the spirit."

Abbie's aunt and Ellen worked for a long time stemming the blood. Finally Ellen stitched the wound. Her fingers were steady, but when the task was finished she sank back and began to tremble.

Luke lifted her to her feet, and walked her away a distance until she straightened. She drew a long breath and said, "Thank you, Storm. I'm all right now."

Emery Dixon was glaring at them uncompromisingly. "Harbingers of evil!" he thundered. "This would never have happened to Abigail if I had insisted that she stay with her own flesh and blood instead of picking up with strangers!"

Then he turned his back on them.

Luke glanced at Ellen. He was remembering the way Abbie's pain-racked eyes had followed both the dark-haired girl and himself before the laudanum had taken effect. Abbie had managed to say that she had no idea who had thrown the knife. But Luke had seen a strange, unbelieving expression in her face as she looked at him and at Ellen.

Abbie, he was certain, had not told all she knew. He wondered if Ellen was aware of this also and just what she was thinking.

Chapter X

Sitting in the shade of a wagon, Luke cleaned and reloaded his rifle and pistol, taking extreme care that the primings were exact so there would be no misfire. Perched on a wagon tongue nearby, Vance Cameron performed the same duty with his own weapons.

The company had forded the South Platte the previous day and was still camped a mile beyond the river to give exhausted humans and cattle a chance to regain a measure of strength before pushing on again.

Independence, now weeks astern, was only a memory. The wagons were coated with mud and dust, and the paint was peeling from their sides. Sun and weather had stained the canvas hoods. Cattle had toughened to sinew and loose hide, and the weaker among them were already beginning to fail.

And men and women also were getting that drawn, taut look that was the hallmark of the affliction called, for want of better name, trail fever. It was a malady conceived of fear and toil and nostalgia.

The trail was taking its toll. Lemuel Barry, an Ohio man, had been trampled to death at the forks of the Platte when a thunderstorm had stampeded the oxen at night. A few days later the witty, likable Irishman, Mike McDuffy, had died of a heat stroke after heavy exertion in a long stretch of sandy pulling on the plains.

And now George Downs was dead also. The father of the little flaxen-haired Honey Downs had drowned during the crossing of the South Platte the previous afternoon. He had lost his footing while making the ford with his wagon, and had been swept away by the current before help could be organized.

Luke had located the body at daybreak downstream. They had buried George Downs a few hours ago. Emery Dixon had read the burial service and preached a short sermon, and had prayed for the safety of the remainder of the company. Abbie had led the singing of a hymn and the widow had screamed in intolerable grief when it had come time to turn away and leave her husband there in the solitude of the plains.

The oxen were now grazing over the grave, so as to beat with their hooves the mound of earth into the pattern of the land. Soon no eye would be able to say exactly where George Downs slept.

Half a dozen wagons had turned back for Independence before the Platte had been reached. As many more, their owners appalled by George Downs' death, intended now to reford the river and head east also as soon as their cattle were rested. They would take with them Mike McDuffy's widow as well as George Downs' widow and child.

It was now late August and the continental divide was still two weeks' journey away. The intolerable weight of distance was beginning to terrorize men's imaginations. Their efforts each day seemed so prodigious, the miles achieved so pitiful.

Cameron, satisfied that his weapons were ready, stood up and stretched. Now that he no longer had the McDuffy wagon as his base, it seemed only fitting that he should throw in with Luke, and add his food supplies to the others in Ellen's wagon.

He went strolling off in the direction of

the Dixon wagon, where Abbie was busy around the cookfire. Her aunt was ailing and at the moment Abbie was preparing a cup of sassafras tea which was regarded as a palliative for the ague and chills.

Martha Dixon's illness was blamed on a cold she had picked up the night the thunderstorm had struck the camp at the forks of the Platte. But Luke was sure that it was trail fever that was wasting her away. Martha Dixon's gentle nature could not endure the uprooting from the ordered existence she had known. Already Emery Dixon was beginning to admit that his wagon was overloaded. Only yesterday, on the far shore of the Platte, he had abandoned their walnut highboy and a heavy bedstead, leaving them to the sun and the rains on that lonely river bank.

In Emery Dixon's heart and in that of his wife they now knew it was inevitable that they must soon part with all of the cherished household possessions with which they had hoped to establish their own kind of living in the barbarian islands to which they were bound. The accumulation of their married life was being taken from them, little by little, by this harsh land. It was too hard for Martha Dixon to bear.

Luke saw Abbie's hand go to her hair, tucking a straying strand in place. She gave no other sign, but Luke knew she was acutely aware of Cameron's approach. She was always aware of Cameron, Luke thought.

The mystery of the attempt on her life on that first night out of Independence had never been solved. With the vitality of youth she had recovered swiftly from the knife wound. Within a week, under Ellen's care, she had been up and around. And now she had regained her full strength. Indeed, Luke reflected, Abbie seemed to thrive on the hardships of the journey where others were failing. Instead of loneliness she saw the beauty and the majestic promise of this mighty heart of a continent.

On occasions in camp she removed the cover from the gilded harp and sat, her head cradled dreamily against the instrument, letting her quick fingers wander over the strings. She played nothing that had ever been composed. What she played, Luke realized, was the music of this land. She played the ballad of its strength and its danger and its allure. Each time he looked at the plains, each time he saw the great thunderstorms gather, or the dust devils in their wild dance, or the vastness of untrammeled grass blowing in the wind, he understood what the strings of the harp were saying.

The journey had also revealed a new phase of Vance Cameron's nature. It seemed to have brought to him a measure of contentment that tempered the moody restlessness in his dark eyes. He had stored away his stylish garb and now wore the linsey and butternut and hide boots common to the trail. But on Cameron even this costume had character.

Ellen came into camp hot and breathless, for she was carrying a sizable bundle of firewood and dragging a dead length of cottonwood.

She had followed Luke's advice and outfitted herself with masculine breeches which she had refitted for size. She wore them with a calico blouse and a blue sunbonnet. This garb had scandalized the other women, but they were only in for another shock, for Abbie had quickly adopted the same practical costume despite the violent objections of her uncle.

Luke came to his feet. He had taken it for granted that Ellen was in the wagon, resting during the heat of the afternoon. "What in Tophet is this?" he demanded.

"It looks like driftwood! You don't mean to tell me you've been to the river — alone?"

"Where else would a person find wood in this forsaken land?" she demanded. "I haven't seen a real tree in days and days."

"Don't ever leave camp again — Not without me or some other man along — armed. Don't ever! You hear me? What you need is a good lodgepolin' to beat some sense into you."

Ellen laughed scornfully. "Is that the way you treated your Indian girls? Did you give them a lodgepoling when they opposed your highhanded orders?"

Luke's voice became suddenly quiet. "What do you mean — Indian girls?"

"I — I understand that you lived with a tribe for nearly a year," Ellen said uncertainly. "I imagine you must have had an Indian sq— wife. I believe that is the custom."

"I wintered with a 'Rapahoe tribe in the Bayou Salade about three years ago," Luke said slowly. "That's up in the Big Rockies. Some trappers call it South Park. I lived in a lodge set up by squaws. They did my sewin' an' housework while I hunted and trapped for food along with the other men. That's the way it always is."

"I see," Ellen said, turning away and

busying herself at the fire.

Luke knew it must have been Tracy Menafee who had told her that he had wintered in the Arapahoe village.

Menafee now came strolling up puffing on one of his fragrant Cuban cigars. He said in his smooth and friendly voice, "A sad and cheerless stopping place. We'll move at early dawn, and I for one will be glad to be on our way again. We must do our best to make up for this delay."

More and more Menafee was becoming a visitor at Ellen's wagon. She made no attempt to discourage his attentions even though she was aware of Luke's glowering disapproval. In fact she seemed to enjoy defying him.

"Mr. Storm just threatened to beat me with a club because I brought firewood from the river," she told Menafee in an injured voice.

Menafee looked startled. "The river? Surely you didn't go there alone? You didn't take such a risk, Ellen?"

"I thought you'd be on my side, Mr. Menafee," she said ruefully.

"I'm afraid I must agree with Storm," Menafee murmured. "It is best to stay close to camp from now on. We're in Sioux and Cheyenne country now."

"Please sit down, Mr. Menafee. I'll have tea ready soon." Ellen relaxed and busied herself at the cookfire. She removed the iron lid from the pot in which a stew was simmering, stirred the contents and sampled the flavor with a wooden spoon. She replaced the lid, satisfied with her culinary efforts. She added fuel to the fire, then got needlework from the wagon and seated herself alongside Menafee on a supply box.

She had learned much during the past month under Luke's impatient tutelage and the gentle instruction of Abbie Wallace. She now knew what it meant to keep a buffalo chip fire burning in a driving wind. She had cooked in biting, cold rain under a storm-blown wagon sheet shelter where she was forced to shield the precious flames with her own body to keep them alive. She had learned to skin and carve game and to draw and pluck sage hens and other fowl. For Luke was a man who lived off the country.

Wind and weather had tanned her skin to a rich, golden bronze. She had long since abandoned the parasol somewhere along the trail and had stored away the petticoats and the swaddling skirts. She had trimmed her dark hair to shoulder length for the sake of easier care, and that had also horrified the other women in the company. She was slender and very lithe in the breeches she wore, but she remained completely feminine. There was desire in Tracy Menafee's eyes as he watched her now.

She was a seductive woman, Luke conceded. And she was wanted for murder. She was harassed day and night by the need for haste. Always she chafed at delay. She had opposed even this day's rest. Luke could see that her spirit was tortured as though it were shackled to the snailing pace of the ox-drawn wheels.

Her anxiety puzzled Luke, for it seemed to him that she should feel secure here on the plains far beyond the reach of the law. Yet, lying in his own blankets near the wagon, he knew that she lay sleepless for hours each night, long after Abbie had fallen into complete slumber. At times this restlessness drove her to arise silently, alight from the wagon and stand in the cool starlight of the plains midnight as though she could thus better grapple with the phantoms that beset her. And at those times also she always stood gazing longingly westward as though desperately anxious to be on her way.

He told himself that her moods probably were the penalty of a guilty conscience. For it seemed to him that only conscience could pursue her now. Surely she must feel that her secret was safe since the death of Dan Slater. But there was no security in Ellen's mind evidently — and no peace.

Apparently it was a matter of life and death for her to reach California before winter closed in.

She still maintained the pretense that her haste was due to her desire to join a mythical husband. Once, when Vance Cameron had been questioning her with casual friendly interest, she had inadvertently uttered the name "Ralph" in referring to the nonexistent Edward Jarrett.

She had realized the slip instantly, for Luke had seen the flicker of dismay in her face. But Cameron apparently had not noticed it. Although if Luke's suspicions were correct, then the handsome, debonair New Yorker was learning more and more about her, little by little.

Her ghost husband and her murdered lover — these likely were the phantoms that kept her awake at nights, staring westward with that need in her eyes — a need so urgent that Luke often found himself wanting to solace her as he would a child who was reaching for the stars. It was as though she knew there was no hope of ever achieving content again. She could only stretch her arms vainly.

Chapter XI

Menafee was talking mainly about himself — a subject of tireless interest to him. Ellen was listening with the polite attention that was schooled into her — but Luke could see that she was forcing herself to sit there and smile at the right moments and to discipline her fingers to the infinite patience of the needlework, when all the time there was shaking protest at this idleness, working within her.

And, strangely, some of her impatience must have reached even Menafee. For, despite the warnings Luke had voiced to the wagon company at the time of the departure from Independence that Menafee was interested only in seeing to it that they wintered at his trading post, the man had made no attempt to delay the caravan since that first day. In fact Menafee had driven himself and his men and his stock as hard as anyone to speed the march. Even Luke had to concede that they had reached the

Platte days ahead of his own best estimate and that Menafee's efforts were mainly responsible.

This puzzled Luke. It seemed entirely contrary to Menafee's nature. And he felt that the members of Menafee's hard-cased wagon crew were puzzled also. They seemed to be sullen and resentful of the way Menafee and Al Thorne kept pushing them. Something had caused Menafee to change his plans, right at the start of the journey.

Luke's false prediction of Menafee's intentions, of course, had not helped to change the low opinion in which he, as well as Ellen, was held by the majority of the company. Luke was looked upon as a false prophet of doom. Ellen was still condemned to that category reserved for women of loose morals. The other women gave her scathing glares and drew their skirts aside whenever she came within yards of them.

At first some of the men, including two or three of the husbands of virtuous wives, had tried to smirk at Ellen when they were sure no women were watching. Luke had quickly put a stop to that. He had taken one man he found annoying Ellen to a devastating fistic trimming. Since then the masculine members of the company had been very circumspect in their attitude toward her.

The company had elected Menafee as captain when the official organization had been effected a few days out of Independence. Al Thorne had been picked by Menafee to serve as his lieutenant.

Only one other name had been offered in opposition to Menafee. That candidate had been Luke, to his surprise. Even more puzzling was the fact that Vance Cameron was the person who had nominated him. He had taken it for granted that Cameron held him in no higher regard than the others.

Three votes had been cast for him. Cameron, of course, had been one. Luke had not voted at all. He had no way of guessing the identity of the other two. It was Abbie Wallace who told him later that she and Ellen were the ones who had supported him.

Menafee was droning on and on. Luke had to get out of range of his positive voice or explode. He gathered his hunting gear. Hanging his powder and ball pouch on his belt along with hand ax and knife, he slung his saddle over his shoulder and walked away, his rifle slung in his arm.

Heading for the horses who were on

graze beyond the wagons, his route carried him past the Dixon wagon where Cameron now sat on the tongue of the Conestoga, watching Abbie as she carried on the cooking duties. Luke could appreciate Cameron's interest, for Abbie had the young and rich contours that were worth gazing upon.

Abbie looked up and saw him striding by. Her glance darkened. Luke knew that his presence invariably brought this darkening in her thoughts. Since the night the knife had come within a fraction of taking her life, this grayness of mood had grown upon her. Often Luke fancied there was a terror and an utter bewilderment in her when she gazed at him — and also at Ellen. He was certain she knew more than she had told about the happenings of that night.

Luke caught up his sorrel and saddled and rode to the crest of a low, rocky rise west of camp. Although they had been in buffalo country for many days none had been sighted. But Luke, with a hunter's instinct, felt that their luck was about to change.

Westward stretched the tawny immensity of the plains with their furry coat of browning buffalo grass and patches of silver gray sage. Here and there rose flat-topped bluffs with eroded flanks of red clay. Coulees and dry washes veined the land, and slashing through this from the far horizon came the river with its glare of white sand bars and its bronze coils of muddy water glinting in the sun.

In the opposite direction, and down-slope, the wagon circle stood baking in the heat of early afternoon. Beyond it the oxen grazed over George Downs' grave. The clean tang of woodsmoke drifted to him from the cookfires. In that lucid atmosphere all the human figures were the size of dolls but sharply clear.

Ellen still plied her needlework and Menafee evidently was still talking about himself. Vance Cameron had left the Dixon wagon and was moving aimlessly around the camp, a listlessness in his shoulders as though this day held no zest for him. Luke guessed that he had again beaten vainly against Abbie's silent disapproval.

Presently Menafee also arose. He held Ellen's hand for a moment, then he strolled off toward his own wagons where Al Thorne and the Missouri Kid and three more of his men were playing poker on a tarp and a blanket spread beneath a wagon. Mack Sledge sat as a spectator of the game, whittling at a stick with a belt knife.

Luke picketed the horse in a depression where it would not be skylined and found a position for himself in the shade of a boulder. He lay sprawled at ease there for two hours, inert, utterly relaxed, half asleep, half awake. But any movement in the vista westward brought him instantly to an alert. Once it was merely a tumbleweed driven by a gust of wind over a rise. Another time it was the sudden flight of a jackrabbit from brush near the river. Luke watched this point for a long time with unswerving attention until he glimpsed a coyote moving off. It might have been an Indian.

Then, abruptly, he came to his knees in a single motion, shedding all apathy. He stood peering northwestward, squinting against the sun's glare.

Some two miles away a barren ridge suddenly had sprouted brownish-black dots that were for all the world like the clumps of brush and grass that formed the pattern of this land. But these segments moved almost imperceptibly — yet surely.

Buffalo! Buffalo at last!

It was a small bunch. No more than a

score. And moving south steadily. They were heading for the Platte and their route would carry them to a crossing more than two miles above camp. If meat was to be taken it must be dropped before the buffalo reached the river.

Luke raced to his horse, mounted and headed away. Looking back he saw that Ellen was watching him from camp. He waved and pointed, trying to indicate by sign language what he intended to do. He saw her lift an arm in understanding. Apparently she was the only person in camp who was aware of his departure.

Luke knew that small herds of buffalo, such as this, usually were spooky and would stampede at the whiff of alien scent. If that happened it would mean a long, hard chase and the chances were that he would never get within shooting distance.

But, after a mile of circling, he discovered that his quarry had slowed their steady southward movement and were now grazing on a rough, rocky flat.

He at once raced ahead again, keeping below the swells, until he was between them and the river and downwind of them. Then he began closing in. The country was broken by coulees and low ridges. He finally left his horse in a dry wash and moved ahead on foot, carrying his rifle.

Presently he peered over a rise and found the buffalo almost within range. With patience he worked his way to a better vantage point and waited until they grazed closer. These animals were at their prime after a summer's fattening. He picked out a young cow as his first choice, laid his sights on it and fired. He saw the dust fly and felt the quiet satisfaction of a successful hunt.

"Right in the lights," he murmured. His fingers were moving with trained speed, reloading. He tapped the butt to seat the bullet, rose to his knees and threw down on a second animal. The buffalo caught the scent of blood now and began to scatter. But he dropped his quarry on the run.

The remainder stampeded out of range. The dust blew away on the hot wind. Luke reloaded, then got to his feet. He stared. His first target was down in plain sight. But his second quarry seemed to have vanished.

He ran to the spot. Then he slowed and laughed. Previously invisible from his prone firing position, a dry coulee with straight, eight-foot cutbacks zigzagged across the flat. His second buffalo had toppled into this small ravine and lay there dead on the sandy floor.

Luke decided to take what meat he could carry with him on the horse to camp. He hoped to return with more pack animals before the wolves found the carcasses. He began working on the buffalo in the coulee, for he was shaded here from the sun by the clay walls. He managed to prop the animal on its back. Then, with knife and belt ax he started to peel away the hide.

All this, from the time he had begun his stalk, had taken the biggest part of two hours. He was hard at his task when a heavy voice spoke jeeringly. "Howdy, Luke!"

He jerked around, aware of his carelessness. An Indian could easily have stalked him to lift his scalp. But it was no Indian. It was worse.

Mack Sledge and another man were heel-squatting on the rim of the coulee above him. Sledge had a pistol in his hand and the other man carried a rifle. Both guns were pointed at Luke's stomach.

"Gotcha!" Sledge said gloatingly. "Dead to rights! I been waitin' a chance like this fer a long time."

A wild greed had stirred his muddy eyes.

Sweat rode down his shiny forehead and into his unshaven jowels. His companion was a bullwhacker named Chape Parker, another member of Tracy Menafee's crew. Parker, a dusty-haired man with a coarse, pockmarked face, was grinning and showing big teeth.

Luke's rifle leaned against the clay wall out of reach. He had left the pistol with his horse. He had his skinning knife in his hand and the hand ax lay at his feet.

"Don't move t'ords the gun, Luke," Sledge warned. "I'd blow the in'ards out o' you afore you took two steps. An' you can lay down thet knife. Don't get any notion o' throwin' it. Even if you was lucky you could only pick one o' us."

Luke straightened slowly, carefully, for he could see their fingers on the triggers and could also see that merciless urge for vengeance in Sledge's face. He slowly tossed the knife aside.

Sledge motioned. Chape Parker dropped into the coulee, kicked the knife and ax away, then moved up behind Luke and ran his hands over him to make sure he had no other weapon.

Sledge now also slid into the coulee, keeping his pistol leveled. He grunted as his weight hit the bottom. He moved in, and the thirsty rage was now beginning to blaze in him. He holstered the pistol. Then, without warning, he swung a big left palm viciously at Luke's face.

Luke understood what he was in for. In payment for the humiliation that had been inflicted in the presence of the wagon company weeks ago at Independence, Mack Sledge meant to beat him to death.

Chapter XII

Luke ducked, and Sledge's heavy palm only grazed him. Sledge yelled, brought his hand back in a clawing motion, his fingernails raking Luke's cheek. At the same instant Chape Parker leaped on his back, wrapping arms around him and clamping his hands to his sides.

Luke was held helpless for an instant as Sledge steadied himself and drove a big fist at his face. Luke managed to drop his head, and took the major impact of that blow glancingly off the top of his skull. The force of it pushed a hard, numbing shock through him.

He whirled now, with Parker still desperately hanging to him. He was unable to break the man's grip. Parker began driving knees into his kidneys.

Sledge's face was twisted in agony. He had broken a knuckle in that glancing blow. He kicked savagely, the toe of his boot driving into Luke's thigh. Luke fell, with Chape Parker still clinging to him. He rolled over and began rising, lifting Parker bodily with him.

Sledge now drew his pistol again, using his left hand, for his right hand was paralyzed with pain. But he couldn't fire for fear of hitting Parker.

Now Luke surged completely to his feet, still lifting Parker with him. Then he hurled himself backward in a diving, crashing fall. This brought all his weight down upon the man as they struck the earth and at the same instant Luke rammed his elbows into his opponent's stomach.

He heard Parker's breath drive from him in a wheezing gush. The man's grip relaxed and Luke twisted free. He drove his fist into Parker's face with all his strength and the force of that blow hurled the man back against the clay wall. Then he pitched limply on his face.

Sledge's pistol roared in Luke's face, the powder flame burning his cheek. But the man, firing left-handed at a moving target, had missed.

Before Sledge could cock the gun for another shot Luke was upon him and batted the weapon aside. Sledge dropped the pistol. His thick arms tried to draw Luke closer. This was what Sledge wanted — physical contact where he could crush and maul and gouge and maim with his great weight and strength.

Luke partly evaded that embrace, only to find himself trapped in a cranny in the wall of the coulee from which he could not escape past his opponent. Sledge's hands ripped his shirt from his body and the tatters hung from his belt. He drove a right and then a left to Sledge's face. That rocked the big man . . . but only slightly.

Now a fist came crashing into Luke's body and its impact was heavy and drugging. Next Sledge hit him in the face, and the blow sent him reeling to the coulee wall.

He fell, rolled violently, and Sledge fell over him. The man kicked at him wildly in a grotesque dance of fury.

Both came to their feet. Sledge hurled a handful of sand into Luke's face, seeking to blind him. Luke survived that, and, as they clenched, he drove both fists into Sledge's middle.

They toppled over the carcass of the buffalo. Now the animal's gore was added to their own. They rolled in a clawing, panting scramble. Luke kicked Sledge in the face with his moccasin.

He suddenly discovered that Sledge was weakening. The man had not been able to shake off the effects of those two smashes to the stomach. Luke broke Sledge's grasp and drove in another body punch.

Sledge lurched partly to one knee, his mouth open and gasping, his head beginning to wabble. Luke struck again. Sledge collapsed to a sitting position. Luke kept striking as the man's body sagged. His own eyes held the primitive fury of a man who had only one impulse left — to kill. He drew back a fist to strike again.

Then frantic hands caught his arm, pulling him away from his quarry. "No! No!" a girl's voice was screaming. "You'll kill him! Don't, Luke Storm! Don't!"

That cut through the saffron haze that held his mind. He twisted around, looked up. Ellen was clinging to him, still trying to drag him away from Sledge. There was pleading in her eyes, and a horror.

"Please!" she implored. "Listen to me! Don't have his life on your conscience! It isn't worth it."

The madness drained out of him, leaving him limp. Mack Sledge toppled on his side and lay moaning and breathing heavily. Luke tried to get to his feet but failed. He was swaying. Ellen supported him, an arm around him, holding him against her while she daubed with her kerchief at the blood that flowed. She was uttering little protesting sounds as though some of the injury and pain were her own.

Luke's mind cleared and he strengthened. He drew away from her. Finally he got to his feet. "All right," he croaked. "All right."

Chape Parker was now beginning to revive. His nose was broken and he had lost teeth. Mack Sledge still lay inert, breathing with harsh labor, his eyes open, but glassily unseeing.

"I — I saw Sledge and that other man leave camp not long after you had signaled me that you were going on a hunt," Ellen explained. "It occurred to me that something like this might be on their minds. So I followed."

"You were told not to wander away from camp!" Luke said hoarsely.

"No one else in the company would care about what might happen to me," she said, and added bitterly, ". . . or to you."

Their eyes met abruptly. Ellen stared puzzled, as though struck by a startling and incredible impulse. Luke, too, was shaken. He had found himself suddenly wanting to take her in his arms.

Then she turned away. He tried to force the thought out of his mind. But something had gone wrong. Something had changed between them.

He took stock of his injuries. He had taken bloody surface damage, but had been more fortunate than he expected. His eyes were puffed, and there were cuts and bruises almost from head to toe, but none that would not heal with time, and there were no broken bones.

Ellen climbed from the coulee and returned leading his horse. With water from his canteen and strips of cloth from his torn shirt and from her own blouse she cleaned the blood and dust from his injuries. Her hands were gentle. There was no shrinking in her from this task that needed doing. For once, Luke stood docile, leaving all the decisions to her.

Chape Parker was sitting up now, but he was a sick man. His face was puffing out of shape. Sledge also was beginning to breath more easily, and he was conscious. Luke inspected them both and decided they soon would be able to take care of themselves.

He removed the cylinder from Sledge's pistol and drew the charges. He jammed the muzzle of Parker's rifle with sand so that the gun would be useless until cleaned.

He looked at the buffalo carcass. "You can throw that goat meat you've been cookin' to the coyotes," he said. "It don't shine with hump ribs. I tell you now that this child aims to fill his craw tonight with —"

Ellen whirled on him. "Stop it! Stop it!" she burst out.

Luke was startled. "Stop what?" he demanded.

"This — this pretense at being an ignorant child of nature. Your mother and father must be weeping in heaven because of the way you've forgotten their teachings."

Luke's gaze froze, but she did not waver. There was no fear in her, though she must have seen the anger that raged blackly in him.

"So you've heard about my parents," he finally said.

"Yes."

"And so I've forgotten my mother's teachings?"

Ellen was suddenly near tears. "Can you deny it? You act like a savage. Talk like a savage. Dress like a barbarian. And you fight like an animal."

"I was left to die like an animal by your

kind of civilization," Luke said harshly. "And so were my parents. I pulled through thanks to men you call children of nature. It was mountain men who saved me. They and Indians taught me how to take care of myself. Education isn't a matter of book learning. Some of the wisest men and women I've met don't know how to read your language or to write it."

Abruptly she subsided. "You're right," she said tiredly. "I have no real justification for saying what I did. Education only paints the surface. Humans never change underneath. They cheat and rob — just as they've done since the beginning of time. . . . And kill!"

Her voice caught a little over that final word. She glanced at him quickly, a startled look in her face. She had not meant to go that far. Then she turned away from him so as to hide whatever emotion lay in her thoughts.

Luke wondered what that word "kill" had brought into her mind, what memories it aroused. Silently he climbed out of the coulee, caught her hands and lifted her bodily to the rim. He swung her to the pillion position on his sorrel and mounted and headed for camp, leaving Sledge and Chape Parker to shift for themselves.

Ellen laid a hand lightly on his bare shoulder to maintain balance. Her fingers were cool and soothing, for the fever of the fight still raged in him.

"Who told you about — about my parents?" he asked abruptly.

"Vance Cameron learned the story from a plainsman who visited the company for a short while," she said.

Luke said nothing. But he was thinking that Vance Cameron made a business of inquiring into every detail of the lives of persons he was interested in.

The horse topped a rise. Luke suddenly straightened, staring. He uttered an exclamation.

Off to the north, an antlike string of moving objects was creeping into the plain from the lee of a bluff.

"More buffalo?" Ellen asked.

"Indians!" Luke said softly.

He felt her fingers tighten on his shoulder. She breathed, "Oh!"

They could make out details in the clear air even at that three-mile distance. The column crept endlessly into view. Ponies by the score dragged travois or carried packs. They were herded along by swarms of what evidently were women and children and dogs. Ahead rode mounted warriors. And other mounted Indians hazed along the great herd of ponies which came — sweeping into view still farther away. Their distant movement seemed only to emphasize the loneliness and wildness of these plains.

"Big village," Luke said. "They'll tally a hundred lodges or more. That means up to a hundred and fifty men, counting the young braves. They're Cheyennes, most likely, but I can't tell for sure at this range. They're likely on their way to make meat on the buffalo grounds."

"The wagons . . . ?" Ellen said, and was breathing hard. "The Indians are swinging west and south away from us," Luke said. "I don't think they have any notion of tackling us. The season's late. Meat is more important right now than anything else. And the Cheyennes haven't painted for war anyway as far as I've heard — at least up to now."

"Maybe they haven't seen the wagons," Ellen said.

"They've seen 'em," Luke told her. "You can bank on that. A big village like that will have scouting parties out for miles in all directions, looking for game."

They headed at a lope for camp. Ellen uttered a little excited cry when the wagons came in view. "Look!"

A group of some half a dozen Indians sat on their ponies at a safe distance from the circle. The people of the company were gathered along that flank of the camp, staring with curiosity. The only Indians many of them had ever seen were the debauched, spiritless tribes of the border.

These visitors were a different proposition. These Indians stared back with arrogance and scorn. They pointed at the wagons and at the oxen and laughed derisively. They were mounted on fidgety buffalo-hunting ponies as wild as themselves. They carried guns and lances. A few had shields hung on the ponies. The majority wore only vests and breech clouts. One had on flashy deerhide leggings and a vest that bore a heavy beading and designs in blue and crimson dye.

"They're Cheyennes all right," Luke said. "They likely had cut the trail of that same bunch of buffalo I moved in on, but they pulled off to pay a call on the wagon company when they sighted it."

As they rode nearer he added, "Young braves. Not a warrior's feather among them. The most dangerous kind. They're aching to count coup so they can brag about it at the next war council. Tricky. Reckless."

The Cheyennes moved closer, their eyes darting over these interlopers in their land. Luke rode into camp, swung Ellen to the ground and dismounted.

Vance Cameron came up at a run. "Mrs. Jarrett!" he exclaimed. "I missed you! Where —" Then he stared at Luke's bruised face. "Good Lord! It must have been Mack Sledge." He looked at Ellen, his eyes asking a grim question.

"Sledge is alive," she said.

Then she hurried to her wagon, brought out a medicine kit and clean clothes and liniment and warm water. With these she finished the task of doctoring Luke's injuries.

Meanwhile the young Indians had grown bolder and moved to within a hundred feet of the wagons.

"Be careful!" Luke warned the company. "Don't start any trouble with 'em. But don't let them come into camp."

Emery Dixon came striding up, outraged. He blinked when he saw Luke's damaged face. "It would be better to bring them among us, sir, so they can see that we are only seeking peace and friendship," he protested. "We can give them small gifts that will prove —"

"They'll figure we're afraid of them if we

start handing out presents," Luke interrupted. "These Cheyennes aren't alone, by any matter of means. There's a big —"

He broke off. Abbie had left the shelter of the wagons and was walking toward the mounted Indians. She carried a loaf of bread in her hands as an offering.

Luke began running. A young Cheyenne, his face fiercely agleam, kicked his pony into a full gallop at the same instant and came sweeping down on Abbie. He was the one who wore the beaded and dyed vest and leggings. He also wore a great gold earring and silver arm bands. All this finery marked him as the son of a person of some importance.

Abbie realized her danger in the last instant. She dropped the bread and turned to flee, but the young Cheyenne was upon her. Leaning from the saddle, he reached for her hair.

Luke's hand smashed down on the Cheyenne's arm, knocking it aside. He caught Abbie, thrusting her behind him. Then he stood with knife in hand, grinning at the young Indian. The Cheyenne glared back at him, grimacing from the pain of the blow that numbed his arm. He spat something in Cheyenne.

Luke answered back, also in Cheyenne.

That surprised the young Indian. Then he also laughed. Seeking to save what face he could, he made an insulting gesture and rode back to join his companions.

Luke glared at Abbie. "If that fellow had ever got you on his horse nothing on earth could have saved you," he raged. "They'd have scattered and vanished like a pack of wolves."

"What — what did he say, and what did you say to him?" Abbie asked faintly.

"He said he hoped some day to lift my scalp with a dull knife or words to that effect." Luke shrugged. "I told him if I ever caught him trying to steal a squaw again I'd turn him over my knee and spank him. It was just about what anybody says in a situation like that. No harm done. He made a good try. He'll be able to brag about how he almost got himself a white squaw right from under the noses of a bunch of whoa-haws. You invited it. Blame yourself, not him. That's his way of life, what he's trained to do."

The party of young Indians were moving away now, all laughing and pointing jeeringly at the wagons. Luke breathed easier. He walked with Abbie toward the wagons. Emery Dixon came hurrying, ashen-faced, to meet them.

At that moment a rifle exploded somewhere across the wagon circle.

Luke whirled. The departing Indians were still within easy range. One of them was reeling dizzily, clutching at the mane of his pony. Then he pitched to the ground.

His companions pulled up. Shrill cries arose. They left their ponies and gathered around the fallen one. There was a moment of silence. Then the braves began shouting again. Now there was a different note in their voices — a savage overtone of grief and anger . . . and of vengeance.

They lifted the body across the riderless pony. Luke now saw that it was the young Cheyenne who had tried to kidnap Abbie, and that he was dead!

Luke glared around at the wagon people. "Who fired that shot?" he demanded.

Nobody spoke.

"Who killed that young Indian?" Luke asked again, his voice harsh, angry.

There was no answer. Luke could see a faint haze of powder smoke blowing across the camp in the wind, but its source was indefinable. The shot evidently had come from the west side of the wagon circle. Tracy Menafee's four freighters stood there, but there were other wagons too.

Whoever had killed the Cheyenne evidently had fired from concealment among the vehicles.

Emery Dixon climbed to a wagon step so that all could see him. "That was wanton murder," he said, his deep voice rolling over the camp. "A life taken merely for the lust of killing. I am a servant of God, a preacher of the Gospel, but it is also my duty to obey the laws of men. It is the duty of all of us. This blood-thirsty wretch should be exposed and turned over to the law at first opportunity so that he can be punished for this crime."

"I'm afraid there'll be others who will see to that ahead of you, parson," Luke said. "The chances are that none of us will be alive by sunrise."

"What do you mean?"

"That Cheyenne belonged to a big hunting village that isn't five miles away right now. I figure we're going to have more visitors before sundown. And they'll outnumber us five or six to one. We won't stand a chance if they really come after us."

Tracy Menafee was standing by. "Good God!" he said, "Are you sure?"

"I'm sure," Luke nodded. "I sighted 'em not more than half an hour ago."

Menafee ran and caught up his horse and saddled and mounted. Luke joined him and they rode to the rise west of camp. There they pulled up.

The wagon people waited anxiously as the two men peered westward. Then they came back at a gallop. "All right," Luke said as he swung down. "Get ready. They're coming. A whole swarm of 'em. We're in for it."

Chapter XIII

Luke and Vance Cameron stood between the wagons. Both of them had rifles in their hands, and two pistols and knives on their belts. A dead, brown-paper cigarito dangled from Luke's lip. Cameron chewed on one of his stogies.

"This is the hardest," Cameron murmured. "This infernal waiting. Why don't they come? Are you scared, Storm?"

Luke gave him a wry look. "I'm full of eels inside," he said.

Ellen and Abbie stood nearby. They wore complete masculine garb now and had their hair stuffed into men's hats. The other women were similarly dressed, at Luke's insistence. "We must show 'em as much fighting strength as possible," he had said.

They had barricaded the wagons as best they could with supply boxes and flour barrels and whatever objects would serve but there had been no time to reform the heavy vehicles into a more compact position, and their situation was far from strong.

The waiting went on and on. The sun was now setting and the sky above the crest of the westward swell bore a glittering, golden radiance.

Suddenly the naked skyline was no longer barren. A horde of mounted warriors, spread in a long line, came riding over it into view. The Cheyennes pulled up, gazed in silence at the wagons for a moment. Then they burst into frenzied, vengeful shouting and began brandishing lances and rifles.

They came riding down the slope to come to closer quarters. A woman in the wagon company screamed. Luke saw gray pallor in every face around him. Some of the men lifted their rifles. "Hold your fire!" Luke shouted. "Wait!"

He stood appraising the advancing Indians. They were now holding their ponies to little more than a walk, and still were spread in a long line.

A few rods in advance of the line rode a Cheyenne who wore the fluttering headdress of a war chief. Naked to the waist, he carried a knife and hatchet in his belt and had a bow and a quiver of arrows slung over his shoulder. He balanced a rifle across the withers of his pony.

Luke suddenly leaped astride his own horse, which he had left standing back of the wagons, and rode into the open outside the wagon circle. He held up an arm, making the sign that he wanted to talk.

This brought a furious outburst of shouting from the warriors. Then the chief made a motion, and slowly, rebelliously, they became silent again.

Luke rode slowly toward them. Behind him the wagon people watched in taut fear, expecting him to be struck down by bullets and arrows.

Then Luke twisted in the saddle, looking back. He pointed and called, "I'll need you also, Reverend."

The gaunt-faced missionary understood. He shouted, "Gladly!" Emerging from the barricaded wagons, he ran with long, awkward strides and overtook Luke. Then, his rusty, dust-stained black coat flapping in the hot wind, he strode along, a hand resting on Luke's stirrup.

"Thanks," Luke said. "I figured you had the sand."

"You believe then that there's a chance?" the minister asked.

Luke nodded. "The chief hasn't made up his mind to fight. The warriors are wild and reckless, but he still has control over them. If we can get him into a palaver maybe we can talk them out of it. It's our only hope. They would wipe us out in ten minutes if they decided to ride over us."

"Yes," Emery Dixon said. "I understand."

"You do the talking," Luke said. "I'll interpret. They will know by your clothes that you are a preacher. They've met missionaries before and are a little in fear of them."

"What shall I say?" Emery Dixon asked humbly.

"Don't try to plead or ask mercy," Luke said. "But don't boast or threaten, either. And, above all, don't try to evade the issue. Don't claim that the murder was justified. For it was murder. That young Cheyenne acted only according to his own code. Don't lie to them. Indians despise liars. Say only what needs to be said."

"Of course," the minister agreed. "Of course, Storm. How right you are. We cannot evade the responsibility. I will not deny it, nor will I defend the person who is guilty."

The Cheyennes were waiting, the young

warriors moving about in savage impatience. The war chief now advanced his pony a few paces. Luke halted a dozen yards away.

The chief was a mature, powerfully built man with intelligent eyes. His chest bore the scars of the sun dance. A medicine sign was tattooed on his forehead. He wore copper arm bands, and a necklace of grizzly teeth. His leggings were fringed with the human hair of scalps he had taken in battle with the hereditary enemies of his people.

Suddenly Luke guessed who he was. "You are Owl Wing, the Cheyenne," he said, embellishing his knowledge of the dialect with sign language. "I have heard many times of your coups. You are a brave hunter, a mighty leader of your warriors. You —"

Owl Wing's angry, dark eyes had not relented. He stopped Luke with savage impatience. "One of our young men lies dead in his father's lodge," he snapped. "His women maim their fingers and gash their breasts. Are you the one who killed him?"

Luke interpreted this to Emery Dixon. The missionary pointed at Luke and shook his head. "It was not this man," he said, addressing the chief. "It was one of our number who fired without our knowledge or consent. We will learn who is guilty and turn him over to the law for punishment."

"White man's law!" Owl Wing said scornfully. "That is nothing to us. Bring this man to me. We will punish him for what he has done." He pointed to the glowing sunset. "We will not wait long," he said. "We do not wish to bring war upon your people, but if what I ask is not done I will see to it that all of you die before dark. We will kill you and ride our ponies over the place where once you were alive. It will be as though none of you had ever lived. You will be gone from the earth forever and tonight."

He wheeled his pony and rode back to his warriors. Luke interpreted the ultimatum as he and Emery Dixon hurried to the wagon circle. The defenders surrounded them, asking anxious questions.

Emery Dixon gestured for silence. "The Cheyenne chief demands that we turn over to him the man who killed that young Indian," he said.

Nobody spoke for a time. Then Tracy Menafee asked, "And if we don't . . . ?"

Luke answered that. "He said he'd wipe us off the face of the earth before dark. He means it. We're up against Owl Wing."

"Owl Wing!" Menafee was shocked.

Again there was a long silence. "We haven't much time," Luke finally said quietly.

Emery Dixon's tired eyes moved from man to man, from face to face. "Who fired that shot?" he asked.

He did not expect an answer. And none came.

"What — what would the Indians do to a man?" a woman quavered. It was Carrie Philips. No voice answered that either.

Emery Dixon spoke again, and now there was the knell of doom in his tone. "Someone here must be aware of the identity of the person who is guilty of this murder. It is his duty to his fellow men to speak."

"So thet he kin be skun alive an' quartered to save your neck, parson?" a man shouted. It was the buck-toothed Missouri Kid.

"So that innocent women and children and men will not be sacrificed because of another's lust for blood," Emery Dixon answered. Again he looked around, challenging them. "Who is the one?" he demanded, his voice ringing through the quiet. "In the name of justice, I demand that he be pointed out. In the name of the lives of all who will die unnecessarily I insist that this sinner be exposed."

The silence was unbroken. Carrie Philips suddenly sagged to the ground, fainting. Only her husband moved to her side. None of the others stirred or even looked at her.

Emery Dixon spread his hands in a gesture of resignation. He turned and walked out of the circle. Luke watched him move to his wagon in which his wife lay on her sickbed. Abbie and Ellen were standing there, Ellen with an arm around Abbie's waist.

Emery Dixon climbed into the wagon. He was there only a minute or two. Then he emerged, descended to the ground with the ache of age and of years weighing him down. He kissed Abbie gently. Then he did an unexpected thing. He took Ellen's hand. He said, "I will not ask you to forgive me, Mrs. Jarrett. I set myself up as your judge and from the depths of my intolerance I condemned you. I threw the first stone. I wronged you and I wronged Luke Storm. It will be held against me on Judgment Day."

Then he kissed Ellen's hand. She stood staring, not comprehending, as he walked away.

But Luke felt a queer, prickling sensation at the nape of his neck. He knew now the import of what he had been seeing. He had been watching a man saying farewell to his loved ones and to life itself.

Emery Dixon was now walking calmly between the wagons and past the barricades. He continued striding in the direction of the restless Cheyennes.

The mass of Indians suddenly boiled with a new excitement. A sound came, deep and animal-like. One voice soared in the shrill, quavering war whoop.

Emery Dixon had moved so quietly that only Luke and the two girls had seen him leave the circle. Now both Ellen and Abbie screamed in unison as they were struck by the same horrified realization.

Luke was already running with frantic strides. Emery Dixon looked back, saw this pursuit, and broke into a gangling run also. He shouted an imploring command to Luke to turn back.

Indians were breaking from the main group, heel-pounding their horses and sweeping toward the minister. But Luke reached him first, less than a hundred yards from the wagons. He seized the graying minister bodily in his arms, turned and headed back toward the barricades.

The Cheyennes pulled up, baffled. Luke

shouted in the dialect, "This is not the man, Owl Wing. This one is a good man. I will not let him die to save the others."

The minister was too spent to struggle or even stand, and Luke laid him on a blanket that Ellen and Abbie hurriedly spread in the shade of their wagon.

Luke turned to the company staring in bewilderment at this scene. "He tried to give himself up to the Cheyennes," he explained. "He was going to tell them that he was the guilty man."

He paused. After a moment he said levelly, "We'll fight it out, then? All of us?"

"Why should everybody die?" a man exclaimed. "I say to draw for it." The speaker was an Illinois man named Bart Evans who was traveling with his wife and a fourteen-year-old son.

Luke heard men begin breathing harder around him.

"Don't be a damned fool, Evans!" Menafee snapped. "Why would anyone draw for a thing like that?"

But Luke could see that Evans' proposal, grim as it was, now was being grasped by the majority. Men, ashen-lipped, were nodding fearful approval.

Scorn came into Luke's eyes, and all of his intolerance of them was in his voice. "I say fight," he said. "I don't ask any innocent man to sacrifice himself for me."

"Nor I," Vance Cameron said. "After all, there's more to life than merely living. We have our conscience and our pride."

But they were ignored. Luke could almost see in the faces of the others the run of their thoughts. They were thinking that in such a lottery the odds were thirty to one in each person's favor. While Luke and Cameron offered only what seemed like certain death.

"Storm should have let the preacher go," Al Thorne said angrily. "Maybe it was him that knocked off that Indian anyway."

Vance Cameron removed his dead and frayed stogie. "No," he spoke. "It wasn't the preacher. I can vouch for him."

"An' who can vouch for you?" Thorne asked.

Cameron gave him a thin look and turned so that they were facing each other. Cameron carried one pistol slung in a holster and a second weapon thrust in his belt. Thorne was similarly armed. Now these guns seemed to loom ominously and huge, commanding the scene.

Luke stepped between the two men. Again it came to him that beneath Cameron's cultured exterior was steel and granite. Few men would have dared offer such a challenge to a man of the known gun speed of Al Thorne.

"We are wasting time," Luke said. "They'll be coming at us any minute now. They're growing restless. Either hold your lottery or make up your mind to fight."

The Cheyennes were beginning to mill around. Rifles exploded in the air. Angry yells drifted. The sunset was fading; the long twilight was at hand.

Bart Evans looked around and said hoarsely, "I reckon it's agreed. We'll draw fer it. Every grown man. No exceptions. An' there'll be no backin' out — win or lose."

Evans took charge. He counted heads. Everyone was present, even the bruised and damaged Mack Sledge and Chape Parker. Evans turned to Ellen. "Mrs. Jarrett, we'd be obliged if you'd hunt us up thirty-one white beans an' one black one," he said. "Or buttons. Or anything that are all of the same shape an' size."

Ellen shook her head. "Luke Storm and Mr. Cameron are right," she said. "It would be better to fight."

"Hell!" Al Thorne snorted. "Poker chips will do."

He walked across camp to the wagon

where he and the others of Menafee's crew had been playing cards and gathered up the chips from the spread blanket.

He returned, lifted Menafee's Panama hat from his head, and counted the chips into the hat.

"Thirty-one white," he said. Then he added, "And one blue."

"This is ridiculous," Menafee said in a thin voice. "Give me my hat."

A doubting stampeder named Jackson spoke. "I'd like to count them chips too. I've heard you're purty sharp at handlin' cards an' such-like, Thorne."

Thorne handed him the hat. "A remark like that would get you into serious trouble at another time, my friend," he said. "Count them to your damned heart's content."

With every eye watching, the man made sure the tally was correct. Then the hat was placed on a wagon seat above eye level and shaken up thoroughly.

"Who'll be the first to draw?" Evans said.

"You don't really think any sane person would want to take a chance on having to pay for another man's crime?" Menafee demanded wildly.

"A chip will be drawn for anyone who

refuses to act for himself," Evans said.

Men edged back, staring fearfully at the hat. In the background a man suddenly became violently ill. It was the Missouri Kid.

Then Vance Cameron walked to the wagon, reached high and drew a chip from the hat. He did not even glance at it, thrusting it indifferently into his pocket.

He looked at Menafee. "Next?" he said.

But Menafee backed away. "I'll have no part in this," he shouted. "You have no authority for this, Evans."

Now Cal Gossard, a Kentucky man, moved up and said, "I'll take my chance. I figure it's better'n havin' women an' the young'n scalped."

He drew from the hat. He looked at a white chip, smiled a trifle, grimly, and retreated into the background. Other men drew. Some shouted with joy and displayed white chips. Others remained silent, keeping the secret of their fates to themselves.

Finally there were only Luke and Emery Dixon and Menafee and Al Thorne.

Thorne walked up with a swagger and removed one of the four remaining chips. He looked at it, laughed loudly and tossed it high in the air. It was white.

"My lucky day," he said.

Bart Evans looked at Emery Dixon. The missionary had revived now. He got to his feet and turned to Luke, smiling. "Perhaps I will prevail over you, after all, my friend," he said. He drew from the hat, glanced at his chip and shrugged resignedly. Luke knew the minister had drawn white also.

Luke motioned to Menafee. "Only two left," he said.

The trader broke into a frenzy of pompous fury. "No, I tell you!" he yelled.

Luke walked to the wagon and drew from the hat one of the two remaining chips. He pocketed it without looking at it.

Menafee was watching him closely, hoping for some betraying expression, just as he had tautly watched the face of each man as their fates were drawn in the lottery. But no man had shown any sign of having drawn the blue chip. There were many, like Thorne, who were obviously safe, but there were also several of the participants, like Luke and Vance Cameron, who had concealed any sign as to whether their luck had been good or bad.

"That's your chip, Menafee," Luke said. "It belongs to you whether you draw it or not."

Menafee's rage had vanished. He was suddenly cool and self-possessed. Driven into a corner, he had made his decision.

"This has gone far enough," he said. "The fool who got us into this situation is the one who must pay. And there he stands!"

Menafee's pistol was in his hand. He was pointing at the ugly-mouthed Missouri Kid.

Chapter XIV

"This filthy little rat murdered the Indian," Menafee said. "I waited, hoping he would be man enough to admit his guilt. Instead he even had the audacity to strut when he drew a white chip. He fired the shot from concealment in one of my wagons where he had been taking a sleep. I was having a siesta in an adjoining wagon. I saw it all."

The Missouri Kid screeched something profane and snatched out his pistol. But Al Thorne, who had taken a position directly behind him, knocked the weapon aside. The bullet tore through the hood of a nearby wagon.

Thorne snatched the gun away and wrapped his arms around the Kid, holding him helpless. Other men rushed in to help him subdue the frothing captive.

The Kid fought insanely to break free. "You — you yellow dog!" he screamed at Menafee. "I done your dirty work fer you, an' now you sell me out, just because you're afraid to take a chance with your own skin."

"Take him out on the flat and turn him loose so the Cheyennes can pick him up," Menafee ordered calmly.

Emery Dixon intervened. "Wait!" He spoke to the wild-eyed prisoner. "Are you guilty, my son?" he asked gently.

The Missouri Kid glared around with terrible disbelief at the men who held him. Luke realized now that all of them were members of Menafee's wagon crew. Even Mack Sledge, battered and bloody and dust-matted from his encounter with Luke, was in the group that enclosed their former comrade. The wolves had turned on one of their number in order to save themselves.

It was evident that Menafee had indeed pointed out the guilty man. It was marked on the Missouri Kid's contorted face. Never more than a perpetrator of petty crimes, the Kid had got his first taste of blood the night he had shot down Dan Slater in a frenzy of fear. That had given him a sense of power and achievement such as he had never before known. Since that night he had longed to repeat the experience. The killing of the young Indian had been done on the impulse of the moment. It had seemed safe enough. Now he saw that it had brought his own doom.

"Take him away!" Menafee ordered. "Hurry! The Indians are getting ready to charge!"

Owl Wing's warriors were moving toward the wagons. Thorne and his men began dragging the screaming Kid into the open.

Luke saw horror in the faces of Ellen and Abbie. And pity for the Missouri Kid. The same emotions were in his own mind, but, above all, was a vast distaste for what was going on. He saw the same repugnance in Cameron.

Luke turned and strode to overtake Menafee's men and their prisoner. Owl Wing, seeing the group emerge from the camp, pulled up and signaled his tribesmen to wait.

The Missouri Kid still fought hopelessly to escape. Froth flowed. His crooked features were a mottled, jaundiced hue. He screamed for mercy.

His fear-glazed eyes suddenly recognized Luke. "You'll be the next to go, Storm!" he croaked. "I ain't the only murderer in this outfit. Yo're bewitched by a she-devil. I killed Dan Slater because —"

He was choked off. Al Thorne had savagely clamped an arm tight about his neck, silencing him.

Luke stood in their path, halting them. "Take him back to the wagons, Al," he said.

"Back?" Thorne spat. "Are you crazy? We can't stall the Cheyennes any longer!"

"Nor can we let a miserable thing like this little whelp go out there to face a warrior like Owl Wing," Luke said. "We owe it to ourselves . . . you owe it to yourself . . . to fight as human beings should fight."

Cameron had walked up. "I'll ride along with Luke on that play," he said. "I say to fight it out, all of us."

"Get out of the way!" Thorne snarled. "It's all settled. He got us into this grief. He's got to pay the price."

Thorne's pistol was in his hand as he spoke, and his thumb rolled back the hammer. But Emery Dixon leaped in and pushed the weapon down, jamming the hammer with his fingers. He looked at Luke and Cameron. "It is too late now, my sons," he said. "It is in higher hands than ours. Only the guilty can save the innocent. You know that. I can see that your own pride means as much to you as life itself, but the decision in this case is no longer yours. The majority has ruled."

Luke looked around. Other men of the company — and some of their wives also — had come surging up to surround them. They were people beside themselves with fear. Some had guns in their hands and were obviously ready to act against anyone who opposed them.

Then the minister, without a word, walked close, and lifted the pistols from Luke's and Cameron's holsters, disarming them. "Pride is a terrible burden at times," he said.

He looked at Al Thorne and gestured. Thorne and his men moved forward, dragging their feebly struggling burden.

Cameron forced his way to the Missouri Kid's side. "Why did you kill Dan Slater?" he demanded. "Speak, man!"

But the Kid only looked at him unseeingly, too numbed with terror to understand or reason.

Thorne's men sent him sprawling in the dry, loose earth. Then they turned and ran in a panicky stampede for the wagons.

Luke and Cameron watched Emery Dixon standing alone over the sobbing Missouri Kid. A wild murmur arose from the line of mounted Cheyennes.

The minister placed Luke's pistol in the

Missouri Kid's limp hand. "Die like a man, my son," he said in his deep voice. "Die like a Christian. It will help absolve you of your sins."

He joined Luke and Cameron and the three of them moved toward the wagons.

Behind them Owl Wing lifted a wild and vengeful shout. He hurled his pony into motion, followed by the long line of warriors.

Looking back, Luke saw Owl Wing suddenly pull up, letting another mounted Cheyenne sweep ahead of him and bear down on the Missouri Kid. The other Indians also brought their ponies to a halt and sat watching.

The warrior who raced alone toward the Kid was bare to the waist. His face and chest bore the black paint of mourning, broken only by one fierce slash of war red across his forehead. He had a scalping knife in his sheath and carried a hatchet in his hand. The feather of a subchief was fastened to his hair. Luke guessed that he was the father of the young brave who had been slain.

The Missouri Kid lurched to his feet, took a few shambling steps in an attempt at sheeplike flight. Then, realizing this was hopeless, he turned at bay. He lifted the gun and fired. He missed.

Then the Cheyenne sounded the war whoop. He hung by a heel on the offside of his pony as he raced the few remaining rods.

The Kid was now shooting with frantic desperation. He killed his opponent's pony, and the animal lurched and went down in a sliding fall. But the Cheyenne landed on his feet only a few yards from his quarry. As he did so he hurled the hatchet with deadly precision.

Luke turned away. Ellen buried her face in her hands. When Luke looked again, it was all over. The victor stood over the Missouri Kid's body and he was holding aloft the scalp.

Now the entire war party, howling savagely, began riding in a circle around the object that lay on the ground, firing arrows and rifles into it, striking at it with lances and hatchets and knives and shouting taunts.

The death of the young Cheyenne was being avenged to the satisfaction of the entire village.

The wagon people stood by, half expecting each moment that the whirlwind would turn on them again. Deep dusk came and still the uproar went on and on.

Then suddenly the Cheyennes were leaving. The thunder of the hooves faded off into the purple shadows of the plains. The dust slowly cleared away. The great silence of the land moved in once more.

The wagon people looked at each other with hollow eyes. They were still alive and they could hardly believe it.

Tracy Menafee, crouching alone in the shelter of a wagon, gazed at a blue poker chip that he drew from his pocket. Then he hurled it far away into the darkness. It had been the last chip in the hat.

Luke lifted his voice. "Break camp," he said. "Get ready to inspan."

"You mean we're pullin' out?" someone protested.

"As fast as we can get rolling," Luke said. "The Cheyennes might change their minds at daybreak and come back. By dawn we want to be miles away, and in a better position to make a stand if they follow us."

Nobody challenged his right to take over Menafee's authority as captain. Least of all Menafee, who knew that this was a time for him to stay out of sight. His prestige was at low ebb because of the role he had played in the lottery, and of the way he had waited to expose the Missouri Kid.

But he also knew that time had a way of dulling the memory. Already he was turning over in his thoughts the ways and means of planting in the minds of the company the belief that it had really been his action in naming the Missouri Kid as the guilty one that had saved them from the Cheyennes.

Al Thorne joined him. "The Kid tried to do some talking," he murmured. "I hope I stopped him in time."

"How much talking?" Menafee snapped.

"He warned Storm he might have bad luck. He said he wasn't the only one in this outfit who was a murderer. And he told Storm he was bewitched by a she-devil. Evidently he understood enough of the words on that reward poster to know that it is the girl who is wanted for a killing. He then said he had killed Dan Slater. At that point I was able to choke him off."

Menafee stood frowning. "But Storm still doesn't know we had anything to do with the Missouri Kid being in Slater's room," he said.

"He can do some guessing," Thorne said. "And likely will."

Menafee considered this answer for a time. "We'll let it ride a while," he said.

"Maybe we've let it ride too long already," Thorne objected. "A little more guessin' by him might spoil everything we got in mind."

Menafee debated it with distaste, for he again resented Thorne's manner in forcing such positive decisions into the open.

He thought of Abbie Wallace. He and Thorne had taken it for granted that after Thorne had failed to silence her with the thrown knife she would expose Ellen Jessup's true identity to her uncle and to the entire company. But, for reasons they could no more than guess at, she had remained silent. Therefore there had been no further need of seeing to it that she did not talk.

"Right now, Storm is valuable to us," Menafee finally said. "We want the girl to reach California for that is the only way we can ever find her father. She trusts Storm and he is the man who can get her there. If we make a move against him it might warn her that we have some irons in the fire of our own."

Thorne scowlingly thought it over while he watched Luke speed the breaking of camp. "Maybe you're right," he finally admitted. "But once I decide Storm is onto us, then he'll have to go. I don't intend to give him the chance to do to me what he did to Mack Sledge today." Then he hurried off to direct Menafee's crew.

The oxen were now being brought in. Luke halted a man who was about to add fuel to one of the fires. "Let 'em burn low until we're out of camp," he said. "We don't want any more light than necessary to give away what we're doing."

He gave additional orders. "Yoke up outside the wagons in the dark and inspan as quietly as possible. Stow your whips in the wagons. We'll use only goads tonight — and prayers."

He turned to Abbie. "Play the harp." He leaped into Ellen's wagon, lifted the instrument to the ground and removed the cover. "Play the harp," he said again. "We'll leave it here for the wind to play after we're gone. Maybe it'll lull them into thinking that we're still here."

"They — they're still out there?" Abbie questioned, gazing fearfully off into the darkness.

"There're sure to be scouts keeping an eye on us," Luke said. "But the harp will keep them at a distance. They'll think that ghosts are roaming the night when they hear what the strings say."

Abbie began playing. And ghosts did roam the night, for the strings began to tell eerily of the terror and the tragedy of the day. Abbie's fingers, wandering over the chords, recounted in music the story of the death of the Missouri Kid and the fear of the survivors as they prepared to flee through the night.

And that thin and haunting ballad was the accompaniment as the oxen were hurriedly inspanned. Yokes creaked in the darkness and chain rings rattled softly as men strained to be as quiet as possible. Swiftly the caravan was made ready to stretch out.

Luke found a supple cottonwood pole that someone had slung on a wagon for some unknown purpose. This he drove slantwise into the ground above the harp that Abbie played. After some experimenting he punched a hole in a skillet of thin metal. He hung the skillet, handle down, from the pole with a rawhide string so that the gusty wind that rattled the wagon sheets set it spinning and dancing. That brought the handle raking across the taut strings.

"Your harp," Luke said, "will play music such as even you could never bring from it."

Abbie gazed at the grotesque object that cavorted on its string, picking out its own weird ballad. She laid a hand caressingly on the gilded coolness of the harp for a moment, then she turned away. Ellen drew her close and walked off with her.

Luke slapped the flanks of the point yoke on Ellen's team and said, "Hike!" The oxen obeyed. Emery Dixon, handling his worn team, fell into line, and the other wagons, one by one, followed them off into the night.

No bugles blew, no banjos tinkled. Nobody spoke. This was flight. This was hope that they would find safety in darkness. Only the stars gave light as the wagons lurched onward.

Behind them the deserted campfires were dull crimson stains in the blackness of the plains. And fainter and fainter came the unearthly rigadoon that was being played by a skillet, dancing on a string at the command of the wind.

Ellen walked at Luke's side. "Your face needs attention again," she presently said. "You could not look worse if you had been kicked by a mule. You are almost as damaged as Mack Sledge."

During a halt called to breathe the oxen after a long uphill pull, she again treated his injuries. His face was swollen and discolored. The aftermath of the punishment he had taken was setting in.

She used stinging alum and then applied a cool and aromatic balm. The touch of her hands was too much. Luke suddenly pulled her roughly against him. He held her thus, looking down at her. There was no way of knowing her thoughts, for her face was only a dim oval in the faint starlight. But she made no move to oppose him.

He abruptly released her. "He was right," he said hoarsely. "You bewitch a man."

"Who was right?" she asked.

Luke swung around and strode away from her. He was angered and a little frightened by the turmoil and the desire that had engulfed him. He owed her a great debt for that episode in the hallway at the Overland Inn. He had pledged to see her to California as payment for that favor. But now he was beginning to fear that, slowly, surely, she was taking possession of everything he valued . . . his independence, his pride, his spirit.

Rounding a wagon he almost collided with Vance Cameron. Luke realized that the dark-haired man must have been there all the time — within earshot of him and Ellen.

He grasped Cameron by the arms, and said softly, "You'll make a target of yourself some night, smoking those Baltimore stogies in the dark."

Cameron did not yield to that grip. The tip of the stogy he was smoking glowed. He drew smoke evenly. "How did you discover it — the Baltimore thing, Luke?" he murmured.

"Your cigar case," Luke said. "I saw it that first day out of Independence."

"Of course." Cameron sighed. "How careless of me. I got rid of it a few days later. It was a casual purchase and I had overlooked the trademark on the lining. He added: "Do others know?"

Luke did not answer that. Cameron waited a moment, then shrugged and murmured, "One thing we have learned, at least. It was the Missouri Kid who killed Dan Slater. That clears up an ugly doubt that had been in my mind, I am happy to say. I have wondered at times, Luke, if you were not the one, after all, who shot Slater, in spite of Ellen's defense of you."

Cameron removed Luke's grip from him and Luke did not oppose him. "I am not your target, Luke," he murmured. "And you will never be mine. But we both may be the target of others. The Missouri Kid may have been following orders when he went to Dan Slater's room that night."

Then Cameron strolled away, puffing his stogy. Luke stood there motionless for a long time. Presently he picked up the goad and stirred the oxen into motion. The line of wagons once more lumbered ahead through the darkness.

Chapter XV

Dawn came and there was no sign of any other life in the land. They continued the march until noon, then camped and rested the oxen during the full heat of the day and rolled ahead again until complete darkness hid them.

By the end of the third day they felt they were safe. And late on the fourth day they came in sight of sanctuary. A stockaded fort with log bastions stood on the flats above the North Platte ahead, flanked by the cone-shaped lodges of a village of Brule Sioux visitors. This was Fort Laramie!

Dogs came barking and children appeared from both the Sioux village and the fort. Soldiers and men in buckskins and in the dress of traders began firing guns in greeting. The wagon people burst into a frenzy of shouting. Rifles exploded in answer to the welcome from the fort.

Luke, grinning, kept the pilot wagon swinging along toward a camp site near the fort and also handy to the river. Ellen and Abbie were on foot nearby, and Cameron, as usual, was walking with them. The girls were exuberantly waving sunbonnets. They embraced each other. Then Ellen impulsively turned to Cameron and kissed him.

Luke's grin faded. Suddenly all the savor of their safe arrival at this landmark of the trail was gone. Futility bore down on him. He wondered if that kiss had been a display of real affection. Or had Ellen begun to suspect that Cameron was not what he pretended to be and was seeking to place him under the spell of witchery that the Missouri Kid, with only moments to live, had warned Luke himself against?

"Look!" Ellen was saying. "Look! Real buildings — with real roofs and real walls. And no wheels!"

Abbie's response was forced, mechanical. Luke saw that this moment had lost its zest for her also.

A wildness that had been somnolent since Independence revived in him. Once again he held the bitter taste of loneliness and the aching sensation that existence was aimless.

An Indian drum now began throbbing

among the lodges. Presently he could see the Indian women in the Brule village, moving in the circling, shuffling routine of a tribal dance. He could hear the chanting: "Hi-ya, hi-ya, hi-ya, hi, hi, hi, hi-ya, hi-ya...."

A celebration in honor of their arrival was starting. Soldiers and traders and plainsmen were moving in the direction of the village, streaming from the gate of the fort, and beckoning the wagon people to hurry.

The wildness grew in Luke. The rhythm of the drum and of the chanting squaws began to reach inside him.

As soon as camp was established he got his warsack and rode to the river. In the cooling twilight he bathed and shaved and got out the charro breeches and the silk sash and the handsome elkskin hunting shirt and the high, white-topped moccasins.

He opened the Bible, gazed for a time at the reward poster and the warrants for the arrest of Ellen Marie Jessup and Henry W. Jessup.

"Witchery," he said wearily.

Then he tore the papers to fragments and let them drift away with the muddy current of the river.

Mounting, he avoided the wagon camp where the cookfires were beginning to sparkle in the growing darkness, and rode toward the Sioux village. There brighter fires blazed. And the throb of the drum was faster now.

He did not see Ellen, who stood in the shelter of her wagon, watching as he rode past. Her eyes followed him until he entered the Indian village.

She stood there for a long time. To commemorate this occasion both she and Abbie had changed to the most becoming dresses in their wardrobes and had done things to their hair and eyelashes and complexions. They had also put their best effort into turning out a tasty supper. There were braised hump ribs of buffalo that Luke and Cameron had downed, browned to the succulent taste that they preferred. Abbie had baked a dried apple pie and biscuits, and there were side dishes of the last of their tinned vegetables and of Martha Dixon's pickled beets and watermelon preserves and currant jelly.

But there had been only the Rev. Emery Dixon to appreciate the food and to admire the beauty of the cooks. Martha Dixon had been too ill to leave her pallet in the wagon, and Vance Cameron had heeded the barbaric call of the Indian drum.

Darkness came and the celebration in the Sioux village was now marked by the screams and laughter of Indian women. The majority of the men from the wagon company had gone to the village to watch the festivities.

Ellen gazed at the leaping shadows among the lodges in the distance. A fear and an anger grew within her. It was a mixed emotion that fed on its own fires, because she refused to admit its real cause. But she could not subdue it.

It was the anger that at last drove her to leave the security of the wagons and walk through the darkness across the flat toward the noisy Indian village. It was dangerous, she realized, and also bold and unlady-like.

But she was drawn on by the steady blare of shouting and screaming and singing. And it was as she had suspected. She stood on the fringe of the village, looking directly in at the roaring heart of the celebration. Rum and whisky were flowing and the soldiers and other visitors in the village were dancing even more wildly than the Indians.

She tried to single out Luke in his foofaraw. There were several figures in buckskins as exotic as his garb who were dancing with Indian women. More than one mountain man was present. But in the swirl of the crowded scene and in the uncertain firelight, and the blowing smoke, it was impossible to identify anyone exactly.

No doubt, she reflected, Luke was one of those bawdy figures. She could imagine that he probably had the prettiest Indian girl in the village as his partner. The fury grew inside her. She assured herself it was disgust.

Turning away, she encountered a drunken soldier. He peered at her in the uncertain light. When he realized that she was indeed a woman he uttered a thick, delighted exclamation and seized her and tried to throw his arms around her.

Ellen fended him off long enough to lift her skirt and draw the garter dirk she wore above her knee. She jabbed the point against the man's throat. As she did so the memory of the day Luke had held a knife at Mack Sledge's neck in somewhat the same manner, rose to her mind.

"Let go of me you — you filthy, drunken lout," she said vehemently. "Or I'll drive this clear through to your backbone."

Her fury carried conviction. Startled, the man released her, backed away and then went staggering off in another direction, mumbling to himself.

Ellen returned the dirk to its place. The fury burned out in her. She was aware now only of a sense of loss and hopelessness.

The open gate to the stockade was nearby, with a sentry indolently on duty. Not everyone in the fort had gone to the Indian camp. Through an open door of a building inside the fort she could see a poker game in progress. One of the players was Vance Cameron.

She thought of herself and Abbie sitting dressed up at that lonely meal they had prepared. She turned and walked drearily back to the wagon camp.

Emery Dixon was brewing a cup of tea for his wife. He seemed so tired and old and worn that Ellen hurried to take over the task.

Emery Dixon said, his voice gentle, "It is good that you forgive me, my child."

He listened to the shouting and the laughter in the distance. "I have been wrong so many times," he sighed. "I wonder if I am wrong again. I have been praying against this idolatry. But I wonder —"

"I hope they all burn in hell," Ellen burst out.

Emery Dixon looked at her gravely. He shook his head. "You too, my child," he said sadly.

Ellen didn't know exactly what he meant. But when she climbed into her wagon to turn in for the night she found Abbie lying there wide-awake, though pretending to be asleep. She brushed Abbie's cheek with her lips, and found them wet with tears. She wondered for whom Abbie wept — whether it was for Luke Storm or for Vance Cameron — or just for her own loneliness.

A waning moon was in the sky. Ellen lay for a long time, watching the shadows on the weathered canvas tilt and listening to the increasing laughter and screaming of the Indian women and the shouting of the men.

Abbie had at last found surcease from her tears and was breathing regularly. But Ellen could stand it no longer. She arose, left the wagon, descended to the ground and stood there in the shadow, wearing only her nightdress. She guessed that the hour was well past midnight. The moon was an eerie broken disc of hammered silver in the sky. The breeze was gratefully cool — and timid, as though it too needed friendship and feared rebuff.

The wagon camp lay dark and silent, with the wind arousing only a spark here and there from the graying ashes of the cookfires. But in the Sioux village the screeching and laughter had reached a climax.

She could picture Luke stalking through that carnival, his tawny hair wild, his face aflame, a whisky jug in his hand and an Indian girl clinging to him.

A sound caused her to turn. Luke's bed tarp and blankets had been spread not far away. He was lying there, his head propped on an elbow, looking at her. His fancy moccasins and hunting shirt lay neatly nearby, along with a pistol and his rifle. He still wore the gaudy Spanish trousers. He had pulled a quilt over his knees.

"It's all right," he said softly. "You can go to sleep. Nobody will bother you."

"How — how long have you — have you been there?" Ellen breathed shakily.

"Long enough," Luke said. "Ever since you decided to quit wandering around and stay here in camp. I saw the way you took care of that soldier."

"You — you were following me?" she exclaimed.

"Someone had to keep an eye on you," Luke growled. "You won't learn to stay where you belong."

Ellen's heart was leaping. She remembered the picture she had been entertaining of him — of Indian girls and drinking and carousing. Evidently he had never taken part in the uproar in the Sioux village.

She suddenly moved closer to him, ignoring her attire, and Luke knew she was trying to read the expression on his face.

"You — you know about — about me, don't you?" she asked, her voice so low he could barely hear it. "You — you know I am hunted for — for murder?"

Luke did not answer for a long time. "Yes," he finally said.

"I've been aware for some time that you knew," she said slowly. "Knowledge like that can't be entirely concealed. And I feel that Abbie knows too. How did you find out?"

"I found some papers that fell from Dan Slater's hand when he was shot that night at the Overland Inn," Luke said. "Murder warrants. And a handbill giving your description and offering ten thousand dollars' reward for you and your father. The Missouri Kid evidently knew about you too."

"The Missouri Kid?"

"Yes. He warned me just before he was turned over to the Cheyennes that I was bewitched by a she-devil and —"

"So that's what you meant the other night when you talked about being bewitched," she murmured. "So I am a she-devil?"

"The Missouri Kid said he wasn't the only murderer in this outfit," Luke went on tensely. "He said that he had killed Dan Slater. But that was as far as he got before Al Thorne choked him off."

"And Abbie . . . ?"

"I don't know," Luke said. "But it's my guess she came across those same papers in my warbag. I had hidden them between the pages of my Bible. I think it happened the night Abbie was hit by that thrown knife. Maybe someone who didn't want her to know your secret saw her reading them and tried to silence her."

"Who would do that?" Ellen breathed. Suddenly she drew back, a horror in her dark eyes. "You — you think that — that I —"

"You could have done it," Luke said. "You had gone into the darkness and were supposed to be hunting me and Cameron. You're wanted for helping have the man you loved murdered. I just saw you hold a dirk to a man's throat tonight when he tried to get rough with you."

Ellen turned and would have fled from him, but his hand caught her wrist, forcing her to face him.

Ellen fought to escape. Hot tears flowed. "Yes," she sobbed. "I am capable of anything — of murdering the man I was supposed to have promised to marry, even though I did not care for him — of throwing a knife at the heart of a gentle girl like Abbie and —"

"Even though you know nothing about throwing a knife," Luke interrupted.

She quit struggling, looking at him questioningly through her tears. "Whoever tossed that thing was an expert," Luke growled. "At that time you couldn't even skin a rabbit without help."

A surge of gladness uplifted her. "Then you didn't mean —" she choked — "you don't really think that — that —"

"So you did not care for this man — this Ralph Gilmore who was murdered?" Luke asked. "But the reward offer said he was your fiancé."

"That is not true," she said. "Ralph Gilmore courted me. He asked me several times to marry him. I could not learn to care for him in that way. But, apparently, to save face, he let some of his friends believe we were secretly engaged. Possibly he expected to sway me into changing my mind. He never knew that it would be impossible."

"Why impossible?"

"Because I knew my own heart," she said. "Because —" Then she stiffened as though he had struck her in the face. "Oh, I see what you mean," she said slowly, "You can understand that even I might have scruples about promising to marry a man whose murder I was conniving."

"Why are you in such a hurry to get to California if you are innocent?" Luke demanded roughly.

"Perhaps for the same reason you promised to see that I arrive safely there," she flashed. "There is a considerable sum of money involved — remember? Money that perhaps you hope I will lead you to."

She tried to wrest away from him. Luke's grip did not relax. "You don't really think that, do you?" he challenged.

She wouldn't meet his eyes. "No," she finally said. "I know that you were not aware that I was Ellen Jessup, or that such a thing as money was involved, at the time you promised to handle my wagon."

"Then why did you say what you did?"

She was a long time in answering. "To hurt you, I suppose," she admitted. "To hurt you like you hurt me with your questions."

"I have one more question," Luke said wearily. "What do you intend to do when you find your father in California?"

Their faces were very close. He could see the torture in her. "Don't — don't ask me that!" she choked. "I — I don't know. God help me! I just don't know."

Someone was approaching. Luke released her and she fled to the wagon and clambered into its dark interior.

The arrival was Vance Cameron. He was surprised to find Luke awake and alert in the starlight.

"Anything wrong?" he asked.

Luke was slow in answering. "Both of us could be wrong, Cameron," he said at last.

It was characteristic of the handsome, enigmatic man that he did not ask any interpretation of that statement. Instead, Cameron got his own bedroll and spread it alongside Luke's. He removed his boots and coat and made ready to turn in.

"There are going to be some sorry men on the trail tomorrow," he observed. "They're all drunk. Even Menafee and Al Thorne. They're now at the point of boasting and demonstrating what skillful men they are. Al Thorne just won a knife-throwing contest. Scored a bull's-eye at ten paces with a throw knife. Drunk or sober, he seems to be as handy with that sort of thing as he is with a pistol."

Luke's head came up. Cameron did not meet his gaze. But there was no doubt as to the significance of what he had left unsaid.

Cameron believed that Al Thorne was the person who had hurled the knife that had come so close to taking Abbie Wallace's life.

Chapter XVI

It was mid-September and panic worked in the minds of the wagon people. Fort Laramie now belonged to that blurred past that included Independence and the Platte and the clash with Owl Wing and his Cheyennes. For two weeks, since they had crossed the low, jagged ridges in South Pass that bore the mocking name of the Oregon Buttes, they had been on the Pacific Slope. But the Pacific and Oregon and California were still long weeks of travel away.

Each morning for some time they had been finding ice crusted on the water barrels that were lashed to the sides of the wagons. And at daybreak today they had awakened to discover a powder of light snow on their blankets.

"Squaw winter!" Luke said. "It'll pass. We'll have considerable clear weather before the real thing sets in. You can expect cold snaps at this altitude. I've seen it snow in July in this country."

The snow had melted within an hour after the sun came up. Now, at midafternoon, the day was pleasant again and the sagebrush swells lay dry and dust-colored and drowsy around them. But there was a cool edge to the stirring of the wind — a reminder that winter was on its way.

The chill memory of that fresh-fallen snow lingered with them. Instinctively they sought to push the gaunt oxen a little faster. The nooning stop had been cut to a minimum. Any difficulty that delayed progress even for a moment aroused explosions of temper.

Only twelve wagons remained of the long line that had set out from Independence. Some had given up the journey at Fort Laramie. Others had turned back during the ascent to the continental divide. But there was no longer any retreating. They had passed the point of no return.

Now there was one watchword that was being spoken with increasing frequency: Fort Relief! Tracy Menafee's trading station on Raft River was said to be less than a week's journey ahead, and it was beginning to loom massively in the minds of travelers as a haven of safety.

It was now evident to Ellen that few of the other wagon owners had any hope of venturing farther than Fort Relief. They all believed that the chances of being trapped by winter in the Carson River Desert or in the mountains of California were too great.

She walked alongside the oxen, for Luke, accompanied by Cameron, had ridden off early in the morning on a hunting trip, leaving her and Abbie to do the driving. Martha Dixon's sickbed had been moved into Ellen's wagon, for her husband's ancient vehicle had collapsed beyond repair during the South Pass crossing. Like Abbie's gilded harp, the last of Martha Dixon's beloved walnut and cherrywood furniture lay abandoned on the plains or had been chopped for firewood.

Abbie was in the wagon at the moment with her aunt. Ellen was alone. She carried a worn cottonwood stick that served as a goad, but the implement was rarely needed. The patient beasts, thin and footsore, responded willingly and as best they could to the sound of her voice. She wore a dark blue woolen shirt open at the throat and the sleeves rolled high, and men's breeches stuffed into small, tough cowhide boots that she had bought at the trader's store in Fort Laramie. She walked easily in the rough going — and with purpose and vigor. Her skin was now tanned almost an Indian brown.

Tracy Menafee, whose four wagons were leading the caravan, came riding back, dismounted and walked at her side.

"If this weather holds we should reach my place in three days — four at the most," he said.

"Yes," Ellen said.

As usual Menafee was neatly garbed, his white cotton shirt clean and fresh. His full-fleshed, ruddy face was clean-shaven and glowing. Sun and weather seemed to have no effect on him. He always had the appearance of having just stepped from behind his desk in his office at Independence.

He was again accepted as the captain of the caravan. Just as he had anticipated, the sorry role he had played in the death of the Missouri Kid had begun to fade and change in the memories of the wagon people. Indeed, the thought he had planted in their minds that it had really been his action that had saved them from massacre, had flourished until it was now accepted as a fact among the majority.

"I fear that the others have made up

their minds to winter at the post, Ellen," he said.

A taut wariness rushed through her. There was something insolently knowing in the way he had uttered her given name. He had never used it before, though Abbie and Cameron always addressed her as "Ellen." Only Luke continued meticulously to refer to her as "Mrs. Jarrett."

"You fear?" she repeated pointedly.

Menafee flushed a little. "That isn't fair," he protested. "Surely you no longer believe the calumny that Luke Storm brought against me at the start of this journey? It is true that I am a trader and that I run a business for profit on Raft River. But you know yourself that I've done everything possible to make fast time. Why, we are days ahead of even Storm's best estimates."

"Yes," Ellen admitted.

"I know how anxious you are to join your husband," Menafee said. "I feel that it is still possible to reach California this season. In fact I am so confident of it that I am going on through myself."

"To California?" Ellen asked.

Menafee nodded. "With two wagonloads of merchandise. The other two loads will be ample to supply the post for the winter. It would be bad business to carry an investment like that for months when there is a chance to move it at a profit. And I assure you I will make a profit in California. They are willing to pay high prices in the mines. But I take my chances. I could lose heavily financially, if I had bad luck in crossing the mountains. You would be wise if you decided to winter also at Fort Relief, Ellen. That is the prudent course. But if you are determined to risk going on, I will see to it that you reach your destination if it is humanly possible."

"Thank you," Ellen said. "But the fact is that I have almost decided that I will stay at your trading post for the winter. It seems too dangerous to go on."

Menafee stared at her, dismay and disbelief in his thin, pale eyes. "What?" he exploded almost angrily. Then he steadied. "Why, I thought . . . that is, I am sure that would be the wisest course."

"I think so too," Ellen said calmly. She spoke to the oxen. "Haw, Brownie! Sandy!"

Menafee threw away his cigar. Ellen noticed that it was bitten nearly through. He mounted his horse suddenly. "If you change your mind, my dear, I will be only too happy to renew my invitation," he said. "I'll see to it that you get through the mountains — somehow."

"You are very kind," Ellen said. "But, after all, Mr. Jarrett would prefer to have a live and healthy wife next summer rather than to know there was a frozen one somewhere in the mountains."

"Of course," Menafee said. "Of course."

He rode away to join his wagons. He was handling his horse angrily. Ellen's gaze followed him. There was a grim amusement in her eyes. The amusement faded, but the grimness remained.

Abbie alighted from the wagon and came with a rush to join her. "Aunt Martha is better!" she exclaimed joyfully. "Much better. Why, I — I'm actually sure she is going to get well." She added fervently, "The good Lord did it."

"The Lord had help," Ellen said. "He had both you and your uncle on His side."

Emery Dixon was farther up the line of march, handling the ox team belonging to the Philips brothers who were down with fever and chills and exhaustion. There was an indomitable quality in Emery Dixon. His rusty frock coat was tattered and streaked with alkali. It flapped about his bony legs. His round hat was limp and sagging. He had a bullwhip coiled about his neck and carried a heavy cap-and-ball pistol strapped to his lean waist.

He had changed. Since that day on the Platte, Ellen had watched the increasing respect the minister gave to Luke. And that respect extended to her. The fact that they all had faced death together in the meeting with Owl Wing seemed to have taught him charity and tolerance. He still opened the day with full-throated, booming prayer, but the theme had changed. Where he once had preached the fear of brimstone and the fire of hell he now thanked the Creator for the majesty of the land through which they toiled. He no longer thundered against carnal sins. He dwelt now on the beauty of mutual help.

When he broke into one of his rousing hymns his voice rolled like a bugle call across the vacancy of the land. And it was vacant — this vast land. Jettisoned gear and equipment marked the wide swath of empty wagon tracks that marched endlessly toward the horizon. It was as though ten thousand chariots of war had rolled onward over those empty horizons. And now the wind was fading the marks of their passing. Carcasses of dead oxen and horses and mules were becoming an increasingly common sight, but they were drying husks in the sun, proving that it had been weeks since their masters had passed by. Abandoned wagons were beginning to mark the miles. Some had been burned by their owners or by Indians. Others stood intact, as though deserted only within the hour. But of visible human life there was none except their own.

Two weeks before in South Pass they had encountered a party of traders hurrying east with a loaded pack string. That had been the last. Everyone except themselves had fled over the mountains in fear of the coming winter. Their own voices now seemed unnaturally loud in the loneliness of these high plains. The screeching of the hubs on dry axles and the crack of whips were an offense against the waiting hush that enclosed them.

Ellen knew that Menafee and Al Thorne were worried. They had expected long before this to encounter some messenger sent out from Menafee's trading post. Even now they were once more galloping ahead of the wagons to higher ground for a view of the country ahead. But when they found their viewpoint and peered westward they only sat hipshot, waiting for the wagons to overtake them. It was evident that again they had found only disappointment. The trail ahead still remained as deserted as the miles behind.

"It's — it's frightening," Abbie said. "It's as though we were the last people alive on earth, as though we were desecrating a tomb. Sometimes I have the feeling that we are doomed to go on like this forever . . . that there is no end to this journey."

She then laughed a little. "Pretend that you didn't hear that, Ellen," she said with forced lightness. "Maybe I've eaten some of that weed that drives cattle crazy. What is it that Luke Storm calls it?"

"Loco," Ellen said. "It's another of his Spanish acquirements." She was silent for a time. "Perhaps it would be nice, she went on musingly, "just to go on and on and never reach the end. For there are always problems to face at the end of any trail."

Abbie looked at her quickly. Ellen again saw the shadow of unwanted knowledge that clouded her gray eyes. Then Abbie changed the subject abruptly. Turning, she gazed around at the empty horizons. "He — they've been gone a long time," she said.

Ellen was aware of a sudden rush of hot resentment. Abbie had been watching the skylines to the north with increasing concern ever since Luke and Cameron had vanished over them. Ellen found herself wondering, with sharp antagonism, which was the "he" who was the object of Abbie's apprehension.

Then she realized the true significance of her emotion. She was almost appalled. But she could no longer ignore the truth, for she knew that it had its roots in jealousy. A vast humiliation drove through her. And along with that came the bitter awareness of the futility of jealousy as far as she was concerned. For, while there would be an end to this trail for Abbie and Cameron, and even for the restless, homeless Luke Storm, there might be none for her. For her any trail might never end. For her California might be only a temporary. stopping place in her flight from the law.

Still . . . the feminine competitive spirit could not be quenched. She looked at Abbie with a new perception and measurement, trying to decide what qualities she possessed that held greater attraction than her own for . . . for . . . She found herself appalled again.

She shouted at the oxen in sudden, gusty impatience, "Haw! Blast you! Haw!"

The beasts, startled, obeyed in such a dumb, devoted haste that she suddenly wept in a storm of contrition. Abbie stared at her strangely, but said nothing. She seemed to understand.

After that she and Abbie walked along in silence, a constraint between them. Abbie was again tensely scanning those horizons over which Luke and Cameron had gone. Ellen found herself watching also. As the afternoon wore on she began fighting a hard fear that persistently welled up in her.

Sundown came and the wind grew bleak. Menafee and Thorne rode ahead to a brushy stream and signaled that this would be the stopping place for the night.

Then Ellen sighted them — moving black specks among the thin scrub cedar on a rise to the north. She felt the sudden, leaping drive of her heart.

"Here they come!" she exclaimed.

Abbie whirled. For an instant all the memories of her anxieties were in her face. She breathed, "Thank heaven!" Then she too masked all her emotions.

And again Ellen asked herself, "Which one is it that she loves?" Again she felt the resentment — and the futility.

Then, as Luke and Cameron rode nearer, the two girls became aware there was something foreboding in the way they were pushing their jaded horses.

Chapter XVII

Dusk was at hand when Luke and Cameron rode into the wagon camp. Both were brittle with weariness. The pack animal they led carried the carcasses of two deer.

Luke avoided the questioning eyes of the girls. "Had to go a long ways to find venison," he said gruffly.

The girls stretched a clean tarp on the ground, upon which the deer was placed. Luke got out his knife and belt ax, but Ellen took them from his hands. "We can manage," she said. "You two need to wash up and take it easy for awhile."

Luke tried to roll one of his cigaritos, but his fingers were cold-numbed and stiffened by a hard day of handling a horse in rough country. Ellen took the pouch and papers from him. After some frowning effort she contrived a passable smoke.

She held a burning twig until he puffed

with contentment. "Gracias!" he said. "You're learning."

She smiled. "Yes," she said, pleased. "I'm learning."

Then she and Abbie and Emery Dixon began work on the venison to skin and quarter and divide it among the wagons.

Luke walked to where Menafee and his men sat around their campfire, awaiting the meal their cook was preparing. He motioned, and the trader arose and came to meet him where they were out of earshot of the others. Al Thorne also got to his feet and joined them.

"Any word from your Raft River post, Menafee?" Luke asked.

Menafee frowned. "No! I expected Pete Moss to send someone out to meet us by this time. Moss is my factor at the post. He knew I was due to pull in about now." Then he eyed Luke intently. "Anything wrong?"

"We cut some Indian sign on our way back to camp," Luke said.

"Big sign?" Menafee asked quickly.

"Three of 'em on ponies," Luke said. "They had been sittin' in one spot in those brushy hills a couple miles north watching the wagons."

Menafee laughed scoffingly. "Only three? Why would that worry you? There are bound to be Shoshones around. This is their stamping grounds."

"I had an all-gone feeling under my wishbone that these fellows were Utes," Luke said. "If so they wouldn't be up here alone. Utes ride in strength when they come into the Snake country. They only head this direction to raid."

"The Utes are friends of mine," Menafee assured him. "They trade with me at Fort Relief. There's nothing to worry about. Perhaps that's why Pete Moss hasn't been able to spare a man to meet us. If the Utes are on a trading trip he's likely had his hands full."

Luke's uneasiness subsided somewhat. Both Menafee and Al Thorne were experienced in Indian ways. "Maybe I'm growing a little edgy," he admitted.

He gazed around. For the sake of convenience, the weary travelers had left the wagons in a loose circle when they had outspanned. There were gaps between the vehicles. This gave more elbow room, and also made the task of inspanning much easier.

"Maybe, just to play safe, we ought to tighten up that circle tonight," he said. "We're spread pretty thin."

"That would mean yoking up again, and

an hour's work fussing around," Menafee snapped. "I don't figure any of these tired people would take kindly to it. Leastwise I'm not going to ask it of them. Utes! You're imagining things, Luke. Why would Utes be this far north this late in season anyway? They always winter beyond the Rockies in South Park where they can work on the buffalo herds. You know that. Those were Shoshones if you saw anything at all. They're harmless." He added, mollifyingly, "We're several days ahead of schedule. That's probably why we haven't heard from Pete Moss."

Then he said, casually, "Mrs. Jarrett tells me she intends to winter at Fort Relief, along with the rest of the company. I told her I consider it a wise decision."

Luke hid his surprise. "I reckon if the others stay there's nothing else for her to do," he said.

He walked away then.

"He doesn't believe it any more than we do," Al Thorne murmured to Menafee. "He figures she told you that to throw you off. And he's right. She knows we're onto her. She an' Storm have likely guessed if the Missouri Kid knew her real identity that you know it also."

Menafee nodded. "I believe you're right," he said.

"She's been hell-bent on reachin' California, an' wouldn't pass up a chance like you offered unless she was next to us," Thorne said. "That means she figures on givin' us the slip an' goin' ahead with Storm."

He let that sink in, then murmured, "You must admit now that it's high time Storm met some bad luck."

Menafee hesitated. "Yes," he finally breathed reluctantly. "But neither of us must be connected with it."

"Mack Sledge will be happy to accommodate," Thorne whispered. "He's had the urge every time Storm has turned his back since they had that fight."

"Then let it be Sledge's grudge that brings it about," Menafee said. "Let it be none of our affair."

Luke's weariness eased as he sat by the warmth of the fire eating the food Ellen and Abbie kept heaping on his metal plate. The venison was thin-cut and expertly broiled. The biscuits from the dutch oven were golden brown. There were raisin dumplings, dusted with brown sugar and cinnamon.

"Not bad grub," Luke finally conceded.

"Hallelujah!" Abbie exclaimed. "We've

passed the test, Ellen. He actually speaks approval of our cooking."

"To that I say amen," Emery Dixon chuckled. "Recalling some of your rather disastrous culinary attempts back in the Kansas country, I will state with wonder and gratification that you both have learned exceedingly well. Fortunate are the husbands who will reap the benefit of your abilities in the future."

"Thank you, Reverend," Ellen said meekly. "But it might have been as well if you had not brought up the past. I say to let burned beans and half-baked biscuits be forgotten."

"I too wish to add my word of praise to you young ladies for your skill with the skillet," Cameron said.

For the moment they were gay. Luke and Cameron filled the water barrels on the wagons, brought in armloads of sagebrush snags and replenished the fire. They sat smoking while Ellen and Abbie finished the chores.

Abbie hummed a little wordless song as she moved about. Like the music she had played on the abandoned harp, the song reflected the mood of the land. At that moment it was a contented, lilting sound, an ode of thankfulness that, for the night at least, they were safe and warm and together.

Luke listened, his mind and body slack and at peace. Then, perversely, the uneasiness came back. He thought of those pony tracks in the hills. He found himself listening — not to Abbie and her song — but to the night itself.

It was silent — too utterly silent. The wind had died. Even the usual shrilling of the coyotes, challenging the loneliness of their campfires, was missing. There was nothing. Nothing!

Presently Luke casually thrust his pistol in his belt and drifted off into the shadows beyond the wagons. He paused not far from the brush along the nearby stream.

Standing there he tried to pierce that blank, soundless wall that was the night. But he was only conscious of the sharpened throb of his own heart. Finally he was unable to say whether it was this he was hearing — or the pulse of something out there in the blackness, something savage and watchful and waiting.

He turned. Someone was approaching from the wagons. Against the reflection of the fires he saw that it was Ellen. He spoke her name and she came groping to join him. She carried an empty water pail as an excuse for leaving the wagon. Luke took it from her, then led her by the hand nearer the brushy stream away from the fireglow.

He had known this was coming. For, like himself, her moment of contentment had been brief. For a time, as Abbie sang and the fire burned comfortingly, she had been at peace. Then he had seen the desperation return. Once again her mind had gone back to the need to be racing westward to whatever rendezvous awaited her in California.

As was her custom when in camp she had changed from breeches and boots to petticoats and a warm woolen skirt and blouse. She had drawn a scarf over her hair.

Never since that night at Fort Laramie had she mentioned that moment of intimacy and revelation. And Luke had waited for her to speak if she chose. Now he sensed that the time had come. And, like that night, she again stood very close to him so that she could talk in a mere murmur — disturbingly close.

"You must go away!" she breathed. "Tonight! At once!"

Luke was astounded. He had expected anything but that. He started to speak but she halted him.

"Your life is in danger," she said. "I know it! I feel it! Menafee knows about — about me."

"What makes you think so?"

"I set a trap for him today," she said. "I told him I planned to stay at Fort Relief for the winter. It wasn't the truth, of course. But it caught him off guard. It was the last thing he had expected from me. The one thing he did not want. He has been planning on benefiting from his knowledge of me."

Luke nodded. "I've been convinced for some time that he put the Missouri Kid up to stealing those papers from Dan Slater that night in Independence. And I have reason to believe it was Al Thorne who tried to kill Abbie that night on the trail because he found her reading the warrants I carried in my warsack. But why are you sure all of a sudden that my scalp might be lifted?"

"Menafee told me he is sending two wagons through to California," Ellen explained. "He offered me his protection. He thought I would jump at the chance. He was so taken aback when I refused that he betrayed himself. I thought for a moment he was going to strike me with his fist. I'm sure he now realizes that I tricked him.

And, knowing it was a trick, he'll also know that I am aware of his motives. Therefore he will try to make sure I do not part company with the wagon train without his knowledge."

She hesitated, then went on. "You are the only one I would trust to get me to California on time. He knows that also."

"What do you mean — on time?" Luke asked abruptly. "Why is it so important you reach California in a hurry?"

She debated this for a moment, then made her decision to confide in him. "I am trying to intercept a certain ship — a ship from the East Coast which sailed for San Francisco," she said.

"So that's it!" Luke said slowly. "You're racing a ship!"

"I fear it's a losing race," she said wearily.

"I take it your father is aboard this ship?"

Her chin came up. "I know what you are trying to ask. You asked that same question before. What am I going to do when I find him?" Her voice broke. "Not what you think," she sobbed. "I love my father. I — I can't believe . . . But I must know the truth. I must!"

Suddenly his arms were around her. He

held her roughly against him. He had not intended anything like this. "Ellen . . . Ellen!" he found himself saying. "What are you trying to tell me?"

She opposed him for a moment, her body rigid. Then, as though unable to resist the same emotion that had driven him to this, she yielded. She buried her face against his chest and clung to him for a moment, wildly, longingly. She was shaken by grief.

Abruptly she drew away. "This is all wrong . . . for you!" she choked. "I have no right to — to bind you to me this way. I will not let you be bewitched by —"

A gun exploded, its white-hot flicker of flame bursting in the brush a short distance away. Luke felt his fingers clamp on her arm in a burst of agony. Something savage and deadly had struck him in the chest. He said thickly, "Ellen . . . !"

Then he reeled against her.

At the same moment another pistol erupted twice in the thickets not far from where the assassin's shot had come. A man began wheezing in blood-drowned suffocation in the darkness.

Chapter XVIII

Ellen sank to the ground, letting her body partly cushion Luke's fall. He sagged heavily upon her. In a burst of reflex agony he got to his knees, trying to draw his pistol. Then he pitched on his face at her side.

Ellen was screaming. Her voice was laden with the overpowering sadness of loss.

The camp came alive. Men crashed through the brush, shouting. Vance Cameron was the first to reach Ellen's side. He had a cap-and-ball pistol in his hand. It still reeked of fresh-fired powder smoke.

Ellen was huddled on her knees beside Luke's body. She was stroking his hair and rocking back and forth in grief.

"Too late!" she was moaning. "Too late! And he loved life so!" She looked up at Cameron. "Everything I touch turns to dead ashes," she said. "They all — all die!"

Cameron lifted her to her feet. He and Abbie walked her to the wagons.

Men brought torches and Emery Dixon bent close examining Luke. Presently he looked up. "He's still alive, at least," he said. "Fix a stretcher."

They carried Luke into the camp circle. In the brighter light Emery Dixon and Cameron peered close. They were puzzled. Finally Cameron slit away Luke's shirt. He said, "Look!"

Around Luke's neck, held by a finely wrought silver chain, hung the small buckskin packet that was his medicine sack. This had been struck by a bullet. Inside the sack were only a silver medallion that had commemorated the ordination of Luke's father as a minister, and a gold-bound cameo breast-pin that had belonged to Luke's mother. Both of these objects were smashed. Both had stopped the pistol ball that would have torn through his chest. Beneath the flattened medicine sack was a great purple bruise as though Luke had been struck with a club.

Presently his eyes opened and he looked up blankly into the faces around him. He tried to rise, but Cameron held him gently back.

"Easy, my friend," Cameron said. "Easy.

You'll never come closer than that one. An inch either way would have done the trick. Your medicine was strong tonight. Very strong. Just take it easy a while."

Ellen heard this. She pushed through the men who surrounded Luke. She stood looking at him. She tried to say something. Then she fainted. Cameron caught her as she slumped down and carried her to her wagon where Abbie took charge of her.

On his return to the group, Cameron addressed Tracy Menafee and Al Thorne: "You'll find Mack Sledge lying out there in the brush, Menafee," he said. "Dead, I believe."

"Sledge?" Menafee said. "You mean you . . . ?"

"Those other two shots were mine," Cameron stated. "I sighted Sledge just a moment too late as he tried to bushwhack Storm. I had to shoot to kill to make sure he didn't pull the trigger on Storm again."

He turned to Luke. "I happened to spot someone skulking in the brush and circled him to see what he was up to," he explained. "I was just a shade slow. Sledge had you lined up in his sights before I realized what he had in mind."

"Good riddance!" Tracy Menafee said loudly and emphatically. "Sledge drew wages from me, but I hold no sympathy for a man who would try to shoot another in the back, no matter what grudge he bore."

Luke said nothing. He knew why Cameron had been where he was at such an opportune time. As always he had been making sure that Ellen did not get far out of his sight.

In the wagon Ellen had revived. "Never before in my life have I made such a spectacle of myself," she told Abbie.

"Sometimes weakness is a blessing," Abbie said. "It is always the strong who carry the heaviest burdens. And, too often, it is the weak who are those burdens."

Their eyes met. "I know what your burden is, Abbie," Ellen murmured.

"Burden? Mine? But I am one of the weak I was talking about!"

Ellen shook her head. "You are strong, Abbie. Sometimes I think you are as strong as Luke Storm. You have not confided in anyone, not even in your uncle, the secret you know about me. You have tried to make that decision in your own mind — the decision as to whether you should expose me as a person wanted for murder."

Abbie sat for a long time looking down at her hands which lay in her lap, her fingers tightly interlocked. Finally she said, her voice a mere sigh, "You terrify me, Ellen. You are so calm about this thing, so matter-of-fact."

"I suppose I have lived with it too long to waste my strength on surface emotion," Ellen said. "I assure you I am not calm in my soul. And I have seen the torment in your own conscience, Abbie. You feel that it is your duty to expose me so that I can be turned over to the law. But you have been unable to drive yourself to it. For you are loyal. That is your burden."

"That is my burden," Abbie acknowledged. "You have a faculty for winning loyalty — and love — Ellen. Me . . . Luke Storm . . . Vance Cameron. You hold us all. I don't know what I will do. I don't know."

She arose then and left the wagon. Ellen knew that she wanted to be alone in the darkness to seek guidance.

It was another hour before Luke's thoughts and memory really became coherent. His body throbbed, but that was easing also.

Meanwhile a grave had been dug not far from the stream. Men gathered there bearing torches and Mack Sledge's body was buried in a coffin made of wagon boxes. Emery Dixon repeated a prayer and asked for the forgiveness of all their sins.

It was a dismal and grim funeral beneath the stars. Once more Luke became aware of the utter silence of the plains around them.

Afterwards the camp turned in. Martha Dixon and Abbie and Ellen were in the wagon on their pallets. Emery Dixon was rolled up in his blankets near the fire already breathing deeply. Cameron spread his bedroll alongside Luke.

"You never let her get far out of your sight, do you, my friend?" Luke murmured after a time.

Cameron said complainingly, "It's going to be colder than the frost on hell's fourth door before morning. What a country? You roast in daytime and freeze at night."

"What is it you're after?" Luke asked. "The money?"

Cameron did not answer. He was pulling off his boots, grunting and complaining at their tightness.

"Now I'm as beholden to you as I am to her," Luke said. "She saved my neck at Independence. And Sledge would have finished me tonight if you hadn't got him in time."

Cameron looked at him now, and there

was no evasion, no lightness in his expression. "I will offer one of the prayers Emery Dixon is always uttering that you never have to make the decision between Ellen and me, Luke," he said. "You are in love with her. The Lord pity you! And may He pity me if you decide against me."

He lay back on his saddle which he used as a pillow and snugged the blankets around him. Eventually he slept.

But Luke lay awake through the long, black hours. A cold and gusty wind sprang up and prowled through the sagebrush, arousing a moaning and eerie rustling in the night. Except for the changes of shift on stock guard, the camp lay silent. Once he heard Ellen cry out in her sleep, "No! No!" Then she said, "Not father!" in a tortured voice. Martha Dixon aroused then, spoke soothingly, and she quieted.

Cameron's words kept racing through Luke's mind. "You are in love with her! The Lord pity you!"

He was still awake when the first wan promise of dawn tinged the sky to the east. The sagging hoods of the wagons suddenly stood out unshapen and ancient against this luminescence.

The refrain of coyotes arose nearby in a thin and lonely lament as though they were tortured by all the cares of the world. Others answered.

Coyotes!

Luke suddenly hurled aside his blankets, snatched up his rifle and two pistols and lurched to his feet. He staggered for a moment from the aftermath of his injury, then steadied.

There had been no sound from coyotes all during the night! And these were not coyotes now!

"Up!" he shouted. "Up! Hi-ya! Turn out! Turn out! Grab your guns. They're out there! Indians! They're going to jump us!"

He ran through the camp, dragging sleepers out of their blankets, repeating the warning.

Men came to their feet, staring around wildly, reaching confusedly for firearms.

Complete silence had returned to those somber dawn shadows beyond the wagons. The coyote wailings had snapped off the instant Luke had lifted his first warning.

Now Luke heard a new sound. Deep at first, then gathering volume with frightening speed. The rush of moccasined feet in the brush.

"Here they come!" he yelled. "North side! This way! They're on foot! Trying to swarm over us!"

Now the Indians broke their silence. They began yelling — a high, quavering sound that ran up and up the scale. It was maddened and bloodthirsty, purely savage and utterly implacable.

Mingling with it came the screams of Ellen and Abbie and the other women and the deeper, hoarse shouts of awakened men.

Then Luke saw the Indians come out of the gray dawn — painted faces and painted figures and glaring eyes and teeth bared in the strain and hatred of the attack. They were running low. They were Utes, bearing guns and knives and axes.

Luke reached firing position on the rim of the loose wagon line. Joining him in a frenzied rush came the other defenders. They were in all stages of undress and their faces were the same color as the gray sky in this moment of complete terror.

Guns on both sides opened up at a range of a hundred feet. Luke was shooting. He felt the solid slam of the concussions of other weapons around him. He fired his rifle, then began using his pistols.

The Utes had counted on surprising a camp still asleep. They had left their horses in the rear and had crept within striking distance during the night. They had used the simulated yammer of the coyote as their signal code. And that had betrayed them to Luke — and saved the wagon people from being caught totally by surprise.

Luke's discovery of their presence had stampeded their war chief into ordering the attack before all his warriors were in position. The result was that in the uncertain light the Utes had failed to spread their forces, and, though they outmanned the defenders three to one, they were impeded by their own massed numbers.

Luke saw this. "Keep shooting!" he shouted. "They're bunched like sheep. Flail 'em down!"

A buckshot gun slammed at his side. It was in Ellen's hands, and she was screaming wildly, evidently not knowing she was uttering a sound. Now she began frenziedly pouring powder and wadding and buckshot into the muzzle and fumbling for the ramrod and capbox.

With her was Abbie, resting a heavy cap-and-ball pistol across a wagon spoke and pulling the trigger. Abbie kept screaming also. The recoil jolted her to the toes each time she fired. Emery Dixon was using a pistol too. With each shot he lifted his face to the sky and asked forgiveness. As usual, Cameron was within reach of Ellen. He was shooting slowly, picking his targets.

The Utes broke. One instant they were sure of their victory. The next moment they turned, dived to cover in the brush. The misty dawn swallowed them.

Many of the wagon people continued shooting, wasting their bullets. "Hold your fire!" Luke commanded. "They've pulled back!"

Joe Prescott, a big, red-bearded Indiana man, his suspenders hanging, lifted a triumphant whoop. "We licked 'em, b'hell!" he yelled.

"They've skedaddled!" another man howled and began kicking his heels high in a hysterical buck and wing dance. The stampeders went wild. One instant they had expected to die. Now life had been delivered back to them. Men, laughing shrilly, pounded each other on the back, babbling unintelligibly.

Luke walked among them. "Quit it!" he barked. "Calm down!" He shook Joe Prescott back to reality. He stopped the man performing the grotesque victory dance. "You damned fools!" he snorted. "They haven't pulled out. They'll be back, and soon. They lost warriors just now. They'll want to square up that debt. They won't be as easy to stop the next time. Barricade those wagons. Quit wasting your breath telling how brave you all were, and —"

But there was no time for strengthening their position. A rifle laid its flat and harsh report over them. The man who had performed the buck and wing, staggered as though pushed by a violent hand. He grasped his chest in terrible pain. Then he fell. Emery Dixon moved to his side. But the man was dead.

Arrows and bullets now raked the camp. Two more men were hit. The defenders scattered and raced to defensive positions along the wagons. They began shooting back.

But the only targets were the elusive, winking spurts of flame from the occasional rifle shots among the sagebrush. There was nothing to betray the source of the arrows that came in a savage, snapping stream. This form of attack pinned the wagon people to whatever shelter they could find.

Full daylight arrived. The sky began to glow with the promise of the coming sun. And now, against this sky, evil, smoking objects began to form arching trails above the beleaguered camp. Fire arrows!

The hoods on two wagons ignited and

the canvas burned fiercely. Luke started to leave the fighting line to organize against this, then saw that his help was not needed. Ellen and Abbie and Carrie Philips and Joe Prescott's wife had already attacked the flames with the fury of tigers.

Using water from the wagon barrels they quickly doused the fires. A slug smashed a wooden pail in Ellen's hand. An arrow dangled from the flannel petticoat that Amanda Prescott had drawn over her nightdress.

More fire arrows arrived. By now the four women had systematized their defense. They soaked blankets and used these effectively. The Utes finally gave up that form of attack as futile.

Luke peered between wagon spokes at the vacant sagebrush from which came a few arrows and occasional rifle shots. He had his pistols in his hands, and his rifle leaned against the wagon hub, but he had not used them since the first rush had been repelled.

Suddenly he exclaimed. "We're being suckered. I should have guessed it long before this. There can't be more'n a dozen Utes out there, trying to act like four times that many. Come on, Cameron!"

He ran along the line of defenders, slapping men on the shoulders, motioning them to follow. "We're being flanked or I miss my guess," he panted as they reluctantly came streaming at his heels. "We're in for a pony charge most likely."

He hurriedly shifted two-thirds of their fighting strength to the opposite rim of the circle, placing them shoulder to shoulder at a point where their massed fire commanded the creek brush to the west and a marshy grass flat to the south.

The two men who had been on stock guard at dawn had taken shelter in camp at the first sign of attack. The oxen, free of restraint, had wandered from graze on higher ground into the marsh and were reveling in the slimy mud, caking themselves from horns to hooves. With bovine indifference they were oblivious of the crackle of gunfire from the camp.

Alder and willows grew thick and high along the creek a pistol shot to the west. Menafee had made another mistake in basing the camp so near this brush. It was now a deadly danger, for it was a barrier back of which an enemy could maneuver for their destruction.

"Make sure of your loads and caps," Luke intoned. "They're likely out there, and it won't be long before — Here they come!"

The wagon men were still settling themselves in their new positions on knees and haunches, just beginning to balance their weapons on wagon spokes and hounds and reaches as the Utes struck. It was that close.

It was a pony fight. The roar of scores of hooves rose suddenly beyond the brush.

"Hold your fire until I give the word," Luke rasped. "I don't want any ammunition wasted shooting into that brush before they come out of it. Then pick your target. When I give the word shoot to kill. Kill warriors — not horses. Horses can't hurt you. Rifles first. Then the side guns. You'll have no time to reload."

The roar of hooves deepened to a resonant and fearsome drumming. Luke could still hear the harsh breathing of men around him.

Then he heard them sigh. For the Utes now burst from the creek brush. And the suspense and the terror of waiting for the unseen was ended.

There were many Utes — odds three, perhaps four, to one against the wagon people, Luke estimated. They had their mature and seasoned warriors in the front rank. A war chief, riding a pony whose head and forequarters were painted blood-red, galloped in the center of the charging line. He wore only a loincloth, and carried a bow ready in his hands, with an arrow notched on the string, and more arrows slung in a quiver at his side and a knife and hatchet in his belt.

Their ponies, as wild as their riders, dripped muddy water from the creek crossing. They ran at full gallop, buck-jumping the sage and rabbit brush with the grace of antelope.

"Wait . . . Wait!" Luke kept intoning. "Blast the center of their line when I give the word. Split 'em apart."

The Utes rode without yelling. Once more they counted on surprise to carry them into the wagon camp. And once more Luke's action had blunted the edge of their advantage.

They were a hundred yards away now. "All right!" Luke said, and felt the push of battle wildness rising in him. "It's a turkey shoot! Point blank. Pick your man! Aim!"

Then . . . "Fire!"

Nearly a score of rifles sent a sheet of gunflame billowing from the wagons. Smoke blanked out vision momentarily, then cleared.

Utes and ponies were down in the center

of the line — perhaps ten of them, Luke estimated. But the others were coming on, lashing their animals. And now they were yelling and shooting. And the wagon men began using their pistols as the range shortened.

The Utes, using their ponies as shields, shifted to the bow, a weapon more deadly than a gun at short range, for it was one that could be fired rapidly in skilled hands, and needed no reloading, no priming.

An arrow glanced from Cameron's six-shooter, its barbed head flicking a streak of blood from his cheek as it caressed him with a wicked touch.

Luke felt the blow of another arrow on his ribs and the sting of a graze. Joe Prescott fell against him, an arrow in his throat. Luke eased his slumping weight to the ground, then moved aside and resumed the fight.

The Utes were on them now. They had taken heavy losses, but they were pressing their charge and were dealing punishment. Wagon men were going down all along the line.

A war pony came leaping over a wagon tongue into the circle. It was the Ute chief on his red-stained mount. Luke darted beneath the pony as it sailed above him. A hoof grazed him. Then he fired upward at the bronze figure that was hanging by the foot loop from the girth strap.

He missed. The Ute chief swung his long-handled war ax and Luke evaded that death only by diving backward in a sprawling fall.

The Ute left the pony, landing on his feet with rubbery agility. Luke twisted aside, rolling as he saw his opponent spring, the ax whirling overhead again. And once more he evaded that gory death.

Then they were caught, hand-to-hand for a moment, eyes wildly aglare, muscles ridged in their faces. They were fighting to the death. Around them other men, red and white, were similarly locked.

Luke twisted, tricking the Ute off balance, and drove a knee into the pit of the stomach. He spun in the opposite direction, overbalancing his opponent. Then he shifted grip and wrested the ax from a suddenly weakening hand. That blow to the Ute's stomach was having its numbing effect.

Luke swung the ax.

He got shakily to his feet after a moment. The Ute chief lay in a welter of blood.

A few yards away, Cameron, beset by

two Indians, fought for his life. A shotgun thundered and one Indian's face dissolved hideously. It was Ellen who had fired. The other Ute had a knife at Cameron's throat, but now Abbie darted in, caught the arm, holding the knife away. Simultaneously she pressed a pistol to the Ute's chest and fired.

The Ute attack faltered. They had taken losses that were staggering to their village, losses that would weaken them in their hereditary feuds against the Cheyennes. They were realizing that their chief was dead, and that one of their subchiefs was gone also.

They broke again — and this time they were finished. The half dozen who still fought inside the wagon circle turned to escape. The retreat changed to a panic. They began streaming for safety into the brush. Some rode blindly through the marsh among the oxen. And vengeful wagon men continued to pick them off, dropping their bodies into the black mire among the placid, uncomprehending cattle.

Soon the last of the Utes was gone, leaving only the litter of the attack. A few wisps of smoke rose from the naked hoops of half a dozen wagons whose tops had been burned off.

Amanda Prescott would never see Indiana again. She lay dead near her husband's body, killed by an arrow. And to Luke that was the worst sight of all in a scene where more than a score of dead Utes and many wagon people lay scattered about. A wounded Indian pony was making agonized sounds. Another was trying to rise on two broken legs. Luke found a pistol with two unspent loads and used it on the suffering animals.

Ellen had sagged against a wagon wheel and was still staring at the ghastly disfigurement she had inflicted on the dead Ute, her eyes wide and fixed. Luke walked to her, placed a hand beneath her chin, lifted her head and turned her away so that she could no longer see what she had been forced to do.

Emery Dixon, breathing with the harsh effort of a man who has passed the limit of his endurance, took Ellen off his hands. The minister was powder-burned and stained, but was apparently unhurt.

Abbie had fainted. Vance Cameron, his lungs also making that same labored sound, was bending over her, saying wild things. Luke now realized that he himself was breathing in that same agonized way.

Reason slowly returned and he began

counting the toll. They had seven dead and as many wounded, but of these only two were in bad shape. The Utes had managed to carry their wounded away, but had left seventeen of their number scattered around the circle.

The wagon people gained strength enough to bury their own dead during the day in a grave alongside the one in which Mack Sledge lay. And at midafternoon they left this place of death, heading westward again with their fire-blackened wagons, and their mud-coated oxen. Grayfaced, haggard men, wearing bandages, handled the teams.

There was only a single thought in their minds now. Fort Relief! That was the magic name. It loomed as a haven of safety in a land that had beaten them to their knees.

At dawn a chill, driving rain set in. It rained for three days. Mud! It resisted every footstep, every hoof. It clogged wheels. Wagons sank to the reaches. One of their wounded died. But the others' injuries were healing.

And now the oxen began to die. It became necessary to abandon one wagon, and then another and to apportion the available stock.

Luke watched the desperation grow in Ellen. She fought the mud and she fought time and distance.

Finally he said to her one night in camp, "There's no hope now that the rest of them will go any farther than Menafee's post. I will go on with you by horseback at first chance after we reach Fort Relief. I'll raise a pony for you."

She looked at him, her eyes suddenly bright and soft. "No," she said shakily. "I didn't realize what I was asking when I first mentioned such a thing. At that time I didn't know about such things as — as Utes and men like Sledge and Menafee. You must stay clear of me."

It was as though that ended the subject as far as she was concerned. But, from then on, Luke, like Cameron, never let her far out of his sight. For he knew she had made up her mind to make the attempt to reach California alone.

It was late afternoon of the fourth day when Menafee and Al Thorne, riding ahead, rose in the stirrups and emptied their rifles in the air. They waved their hats exultantly.

"Fort Relief!" a weary stampeder yelled. "They've sighted it! We're safe, thank God!"

The travelers left the wagons and ran

ahead to join Menafee. They were cheering wildly.

Luke and Ellen were the only ones who remained with the oxen. "You were right," she said. "This is the end of the journey for them, for this season at least."

"We'll pull out tonight after the rest are asleep," he said. "I'll help myself to Cameron's horse for you to ride."

She swung around, surprised. "No," she said. "No! I can't force such a risk on you. I told you that. I'll travel with Menafee's wagons if he sends them through."

Luke shook his head firmly. "Be ready when I give the word tonight," he said. "I'll round up all I can in the way of food, and will try to have a packhorse."

They both became aware of the sudden silence. The shouting had died. The people on the skyline only stood, staring. Luke and Ellen looked at each other. Then they ran to join them.

Raft River valley lay before them under a pall of gray clouds. On a bare flat near the stream stood the fire-smudged, roof-fallen ruins of the log-and-mud buildings that had been Menafee's trading post.

Fort Relief was no more. The Utes had passed this way before their attack on the wagon caravan.

Luke caught up his horse, saddled and rode nearer, along with Menafee and Al Thorne. They pulled up in the sagging stockade, gazing at the charred, scalped, coyote-ravaged objects that had once been Menafee's traders and their Indian wives.

Menafee ignored these gruesome forms. "But the Utes were friendly," he kept saying in choleric rage.

He rode to his burned trading post, glaring at the debris. "Everything of value stolen, and the rest burned," he raged. He smashed a fist in a palm. "This is going to cost me a pretty penny!"

Luke twisted in the saddle to stare at him. His expression caused Menafee to haul his horse sharply around, his hand moving toward the breast of his coat, where he carried a pistol in a shoulder holster.

"It's time to worry about those people we got out there," Luke said. "Not about money. Chances are you'll be counting your pennies in hell before we get out of this."

Menafee's pale fury did not subside. But he let his hand fall to the saddlehorn again, and turned his back on Luke.

They rode back to the wagons. "Drive on!" Luke said. "We can make another mile or two before dark."

Men stumbled numbly to obey. They were realizing with a slowly mounting horror that there was now no safety for them except beyond the California mountains. The wagons crunched ahead once more, the oxen doing their best to respond to the urging of men who were now beset by complete fear.

Luke took charge of Ellen's team. He looked at her, then lifted her to the saddle of his horse which walked along at his side.

She rode limp and silent for a time. Finally she shook her head. "If Fort Relief had been in existence they would have been reasonably safe there for the winter," she said, as though answering his unspoken question. "But now they need help. There are sick people to be looked after. And there will be more. We must stay with them."

"This ship your —"

She halted him abruptly. "We can't leave Abbie now," she said positively. "Nor her uncle. Nor Vance Cameron. It would be desertion — desertion to save ourselves. You know that."

It was the answer Luke had expected. But he strode along, wrestling with a bitter problem. Again one of her first thoughts had been for Cameron. Apparently she still had no suspicion that she was the reason he was accompanying them on this journey.

The whips crackled in the raw, bleak twilight. Fort Relief fell slowly astern. Men kept looking back and were easier in mind when those ghostly ruins at last were hidden in the deepening dusk.

At full dark they made a dismal, nervous camp on a windswept rocky ridge that would serve as a good defensive position in case of attack. There, at Luke's insistence, they selected four wagons that were in the best condition and stocked them with supplies from Menafee's merchandise. Menafee kept account of every ounce of flour and sugar and rice and said he would see to it that they paid for it.

They cached what was left among the rocks. At daybreak they set out toward the Humboldt River.

The following morning, fifteen miles farther along, they found one of their number, John Rush, a soft-voiced little stampeder from the hills of Tennessee, dead with a Ute arrow in his body. Rush had been on stock guard. And three oxen were done for, hamstrung or skewered by arrows. Raiders had crept in just before daybreak.

Now they fled down the trail toward the Humboldt with death at their wagon hubs.

Chapter XIX

Luke braced his heels, heaving at the wagon with all his strength to assist the oxen. The muscles stood out on his long jaws, and veins banded his temples. His eyes had receded deeper into the leanness of his face. A stubble of wiry, sandy beard glinted in the thin sunlight. His hunting shirt — the gaudy one — was torn and alkali-streaked. The last of his moccasins had long since worn out, and he was forced to reconcile himself to the hide boots that he despised.

Side by side with him Vance Cameron and Emery Dixon also strained to keep the wagon moving. They too were gaunt, unshaven and hollow-eyed. Dust rose about them, dry and choking; it lay deep in the creases of their clothes and in the lines of their faces. The oxen were bone racks now, and coated with alkali.

Ahead, Abbie and Ellen handled the team, encouraging the animals with voice and at times with prayer. And they too often put their shoulders to the wagon alongside the men.

On this bleak day they wore skirts — the same comely dress-up affairs in printed cotton that they had found no opportunity to don since Fort Laramie.

Strangely enough it had been Emery Dixon who had advised this attire for the day's journey instead of the denim breeches and butternut shirts that was their customary trail garb. "It is going to be a windy day," the minister had said with a reckless twinkle in his eye. "And also a day when men's minds must be kept off their troubles."

His wife stared at him in mock horror. "Emery Dixon!" she exclaimed. "You are a scandal!"

Then Martha Dixon laughed and kissed her husband. She had been up and about since Fort Relief. Where others were weakening she seemed to gain in endurance each day, as though their need was her strength. In shedding the last of the belongings that had been a part of her past life she seemed to have also shed the sorrow of their loss.

"Beauty was created to be seen," Emery Dixon said shamelessly.

He then turned to Ellen and bowed gallantly. "I speak from my experience, I assure you. I recall another windy day a long time ago on the Kansas prairie, Mrs. Jarrett."

"Uncle!" Abbie gasped. "You are positively shocking. I will pray for you tonight."

But it was now midafternoon and there was no longer such gaiety to buoy them. The November wind Emery Dixon had mentioned was an enemy. It was an arid wind as dry as sand, and it was cold and hostile and fought to hold them back.

For, of all the two thousand miles they had traveled, this day's distances were the worst. Around them lay the weird and lifeless Carson Sink, its white playas and alkali-powdered flats reflecting the pale sun. Now only three wagons remained and these carried six ill and exhausted members of the party. Only ten of them were still on their feet.

They had started this forty-mile waterless march across the sink at dawn the previous morning after spending a precious day at Humboldt Slough to permit the oxen to regain a measure of strength. They had loaded one wagon with marsh grass and had filled the water barrels and canteens.

Now the last of the grass had been eaten by the oxen and the water was gone. The Carson River where they found find fresh water and ample graze was still half a dozen miles away and the oxen were failing fast.

At times what was palpably a great mountain range was miraged into view above the horizon ahead, standing there, in a low, jagged, purple-gray line that they had mistaken for clouds until Luke spoke.

"The California mountains," he said. "They call them the Sierra Nevada. There's where you'll find your gold."

Luke could see that the higher peaks carried snow but that the lower passes seemed still to be clear.

"Maybe our luck will hold," he said.

In that translucent light the Sierras at times seemed so wonderfully near that the end of the journey appeared as good as accomplished. Then the thin mist would close in and the great mountains would recede maddeningly from sight, leaving them on the awful treadmill in the sink where they felt they were making no progress.

Then the fear would rise gorgingly, and they would instinctively try to push the oxen a little faster. And now, one by one, the oxen were dying.

All around them lay the evidence of their danger. It was as though a great army had broken into panicky flight, stampeding and throwing away all its equipment. The path to the Carson was littered with the mummified carcasses of oxen and with abandoned wagons and boxes and trunks and gear left by travelers who had run this gantlet earlier in the year.

Now they were the last — and the silence was vast and mocking. And waiting!

Emery Dixon sagged to hands and knees, his lungs heaving, half-sobbing in his despair. But Luke and Cameron kept the wagon in motion until it reached firmer going. Then they returned, lifted the minister to his feet and steadied him until he had revived, and when the next crisis came he put his shoulder once more to the wagon, side by side with them.

Luke looked at him wonderingly and said from dry lips, "You mule-headed pulpit-pounder! Why don't you quit? Why don't you ride in the wagons with the others that have given up?" But Emery Dixon would not quit.

Both Luke's sorrel and Cameron's black had been killed by Piutes in a raid many miles to the east on the Humboldt, but the saddle mounts of Menafee and Thorne had survived. They were riding them now. The horses were thin, but in far better condition than the oxen. Neither Menafee nor Thorne had ever offered to turn over their mounts to exhausted men. Only rarely had they given a hand with the wagons.

But Menafee was no longer well groomed and affable. He had changed to a bitter, edgy, unkempt man who was torn between fear and greed. His need for self-preservation urged him to desert the creeping wagons with their burden of exhausted humans and head for those mountain passes and safety in California before it was too late. But he could not bring himself to the point of losing sight of Ellen, now that the end of the journey was so tantalizingly near. He and Thorne had discussed the probability that her father had escaped from Baltimore by ship, and that their meeting place was to be San Francisco. But they had no way of knowing if their guess was accurate.

"We could go on over the pass and wait for them to reach Hangtown and trail her from there on," he had said to Thorne. "We might even go to San Francisco and intercept her there."

"We'll stay with 'em until sure they're

going by way of Hangtown," Thorne had snapped. "She and Storm might try to give us the slip. As far as Frisco goes, that's hopeless. She may never go there. Maybe her father made the trip by wagon earlier in the year instead of by ship. That means they might meet in any one of a hundred places. Only she knows for sure. We can't take a chance on losing her now after what we've been through."

Avarice bound them to stay within sight of Ellen, and mutual distrust held them to each other, for both knew that one would desert the other if it was to his advantage. In Menafee's case the financial greed had become even greater, for this journey had proved disastrous. The loss of his Raft River trading station had been a hard blow to his resources. Now the last of his ox teams were dying, and the merchandise he had tried to carry beyond Fort Relief had been jettisoned to lighten the wagons and make room for the exhausted and ailing.

New disaster struck. One of the wagons, driven by Pete Rasmussen, veered off the route Luke was piloting, lured by the promise of more level going. But it was a trap. The wagon broke through the salt crust of an alkali sink, into yellow mud that seemed bottomless. It slowly, relentlessly began sucking the wagon down.

Luke and Cameron and others, racing to the rescue, cut the trembling oxen free and got them to safety before they mired, but the wagon was beyond saving. They moved the two sick passengers in with the patients in the remaining two wagons, and salvaged what food they could. Then they plodded ahead again.

Abbie looked back at the abandoned wagon which was now tilted drunkenly, like a ship sinking into the whiteness of the alkali flat. Suddenly she buried her face in her hands and began to weep.

Cameron was instantly at her side. He took her hand as he would a child's who needed comfort. "There, there!" he kept saying huskily. "There, there!"

Abbie looked up at him and her tears faded. Slowly she drew her hand away. Luke saw the stony neutrality that she had always shown to Cameron return to her eyes. "I'm all right now," she said. "I'm sorry."

Cameron turned away, his mouth set woodenly against any reflection of his thoughts, his dark eyes blank and dead. But Luke sensed the seethe of emotion that was back of that mask. They were all nearing the breaking point.

Al Thorne's saddle horse, a bay that was growing foot-heavy, stumbled over a small rock, fell to its knees, then lurched forward and pitched Thorne to the ground. Thorne came to his feet, his teeth showing in a wild snarl of unbridled temper, his six-shooter in his hand. All his killer madness was blazing in him, and he would have shot the horse dead to wantonly satisfy his anger, even though it left him afoot. Luke had seen such displays of temper in other men in the past. He sensed what might happen even before Thorne had made his move.

Luke snatched his own pistol from its holster and fired. The bullet tore into the earth a yard from Thorne, sending a stinging spray of salt and alkali grit into his face.

"No!" Luke shouted. "No!"

Thorne, startled, held his fire. He wheeled around. The lust to strike was still in him. He started to swing his pistol in Luke's direction. But the smoking gun in Luke's hand stopped him.

He poised in that position for a moment, estimating his chances. He decided against it. Rising to his feet, he holstered his six-shooter, swung angrily into the saddle and raked the horse vengefully with the spur he wore on his left boot. He rode ahead without looking back.

Luke put away his pistol. "We'll likely need that horse later on," he said to Ellen and the others who were watching, a trifle white-faced.

"You seem to be a little sudden with the gun yourself when the occasion demands," Cameron remarked. "That is another item Thorne will take into account in his black ledger, my friend."

They toiled onward. Presently Cameron spoke again. "Storm, what are your plans after this trip is ended — if we live to see the end of it?"

"Plans?" Luke was aware of a bleak emptiness, of a complete hopelessness. "Plans? I hadn't figured. Oregon maybe. It's a green country. Or I might linger in California. Buy me some new foofaraw an' live easy for a spell. They make good wine, these Californios, I tell you now. Rum don't shine with it. They don't fret about life, an' time is just something to spend easy an' slow. The señoritas are pert an' sassy. Then ag'in, this child might take a notion to sun his moccasins in Taos ag'in an' start makin' dust along the Gila, or maybe go by way o' the Spanish trail."

It was the first time since that day far

back on the Platte River when Ellen had reminded him of his dead parents that he had lapsed into the jargon of the mountain men. And he had let the old swaggering wildness come back into his face.

And once again Ellen turned and was gazing at him with that same protest in her eyes. "Stop this boasting of wine and woman!" she burst out. "This — this eternal roaming — wasting your life. This — this —"

She was suddenly almost in tears. Finally she said shakily, "I'm sorry. I had no right to say that. Please forget it."

Emery Dixon placed an arm around her shoulders. "I know how you feel, my dear," he said. "We all share the same emotion. We have been through so much together that, if we survive, the parting will be difficult when the time comes to go our separate ways. But part we must. Your husband will be happy, Mrs. Jarrett, when you —"

Ellen suddenly drew away from him. "I have no husband," she said. "My name is not Jarrett. I am not married."

"Ellen!" Abbie cried protestingly.

"I can't live this way any longer, Abbie," Ellen said. "I can't let your uncle believe things about me that are not true. You have known for a long time. I do not know why you have kept my secret, Abbie, except that it is not in your nature to accuse or to expose."

She looked at Emery Dixon. "I am a fugitive from the law," she said flatly, irrevocably. "I am wanted for murder."

"Murder?" The missionary and his wife were horrified.

At that moment all of the oxen in the yokes aroused from their stumbling lethargy. They snuffled the wind. Then their pace quickened. They broke into a shuffling run, dragging the wagons into wild motion.

"Let 'em run!" Luke yelled. "There's no stopping 'em anyway. They've smelled the river. Water an' grass. We're near the Carson! We've made it! We're across the sink!" Humans too began running, galvanized by the realization that the journey through the valley of death was over.

Chapter XX

A mile farther on, the frantic cattle raced knee-deep into a clear, rushing stream, the source of which was in the great mountains to the west.

It was past nightfall by the time the camp had been made and a meal prepared. The successful crossing of the sink was an invigorating tonic on the spirits of the company. It also worked wonders with the ailing. Clint and Bart Philips, the brothers who had been ill for so long, were back on their feet and eating with the hunger of men whose troubles had been mainly in their minds. Others too were showing such swift improvement that Luke's hopes arose.

It was taken for granted that the company would remain at the meadows for a day or two to recuperate. But Luke said reluctantly, "Get all the rest you can tonight. We must stretch out at first daybreak."

"Daybreak?" Carrie Philips protested. "We're in no shape to —"

Luke jerked a thumb in the direction of the mountains. "We're on borrowed time already," he said. "This weather can't hold forever. It's still a week's travel to Carson Pass for most people. We've got to do better. Someday, and soon, it's going to start snowing up there."

That dampened their spirits. And at Ellen's wagon there had been no light-heartedness at all. Hardly a word had been spoken since she had told Emery Dixon that she was wanted by the law for complicity in a murder. The missionary and his wife still wore that stunned look on their faces. Abbie, grave-eyed, remained silent. Vance Cameron was as inscrutable as ever.

Luke waited. He was certain Ellen had not said all that she had intended to tell them.

She and Abbie finished the last of the camp chores. She removed her gingham apron and brushed at her hair. She gazed around the camp. Menafee and his men were nearer the stream, a hundred yards away, and all of them were still gathered there eating. None of the other members of the company were within earshot.

Then she faced Emery Dixon. "My real

name is Ellen Jessup," she said, keeping her voice low. "My father is Henry Jessup, of Baltimore. He and I are charged with bringing about the murder of a bank clerk named Ralph Gilmore to cover up the embezzlement of some two hundred thousand dollars from the bank of which my father was president."

"I recollect hearing of the case." Emery Dixon nodded reluctantly. "But why are you making this confession, Ellen? Would it not be better to place yourself in the hands of the law?"

"Confession is not the word," Ellen said, her face rigid and without emotion. "It is merely my story. I feel that you are entitled to know who I really am. And . . . and I also am entitled to see to it that you hear all the truth, even though you are under no obligation to believe me."

She turned now and looked at Luke. Her voice deepened with the stir of the racing currents that she was trying to keep beneath the surface. "Above all," she said, "I want you, Luke, to hear what I have to say.

"I am accused of conniving the murder of a man whom I led on to his death by promises to marry him. I never made any such promises. I was not in love with Ralph Gilmore and did not encourage his attentions. The truth is that I rather disliked him. I had told him that it would be better if he did not try to see me again. That was several weeks before all this affair came up."

Her voice began to shake a little. "The night of the — the murder, I was in my room at our home, reading, and my father was in his library downstairs, where he often worked in the evenings on business matters. It was Saturday evening which was the housekeeper's night out. There was no one else in the house.

"I heard a carriage stop at our driveway. I glanced around the curtains and saw Ralph Gilmore walking to the door. I heard him knock, heard my father admit him. They went into the library, talking in a friendly manner. I had an impression that Ralph's appearance was unexpected. In other words that my father had not sent for him. I thought nothing more of it, taking it for granted that some errand concerning the bank had brought Ralph there."

She paused, gazing into the fire, and Luke knew she was seeing these things in her memory. "And that is all I know," she said slowly. "I fell asleep not long after. It was morning before I discovered that my father was missing. There were no signs of a struggle. Nothing! And on the following day, which was Monday, examiners learned that there was a shortage in my father's accounts at the bank. Then, four weeks later, they found the remains of Ralph Gilmore's body in the bay. They had previously found a letter in his room saying that if anything happened to him my father and I should be held to account for our actions."

"And so you fled to escape arrest?" Emery Dixon asked gravely.

"Yes. But there were other reasons. Witnesses told the authorities they had seen my father driving a carriage out of Baltimore late that Saturday night. My father was easy to recognize. He was a big, distinguished-looking man with a graying Vandyke beard and sideburns. He always wore a gray frock coat and a gray cloth top hat of a kind that was in style a generation ago and which he preferred over the silk hats that most bankers wear nowadays.

"The carriage and team were found abandoned in a wood miles from town a few days later. There were dried bloodstains, suggesting that a body had been carried somewhere and abandoned. But the authorities had no way of knowing where my father had gone.

"Meanwhile I discovered that I was being watched. I did not know at the time that the investigators had found the letter in Ralph Gilmore's room, and that they believed Ralph had been done away with and that I would eventually lead them to my father's hiding place."

"There are others who figure the same way," Luke said. He did not look in Cameron's direction.

"The bank had been forced to close," Ellen went on. "Now creditors moved in, seized our home and everything they could lay hands on. They even took my clothes. However, I had more than two thousand dollars in cash in my own private account that I managed to hold onto, as well as some jewelry that I sold later. It was this that financed me on this journey.

"I moved to a little rooming house in a modest district in Baltimore. I was still being watched, but an old sea captain named Jonathan Tremaine, who had been a friend of my father's managed to come to me one evening, unknown to the authorities. He said my father had done him a very great favor at some time in the past and he had never forgotten it.

"Captain Tremaine was master of an old

square-rigger that hauled lumber from the mills in Maine. He had just arrived in Baltimore with a cargo. But it turned out that his previous cargo had been delivered in New York Harbor. That had been some weeks previously. His ship had been docked in the East River, discharging lumber. At a berth nearby was a small bark named the *Whiton* which had finished loading and was casting off.

"The *Whiton* was crowded with gold stampeders and freight, for, small as she was, she was sailing for the California gold fields by way of Cape Horn."

Ellen waited a moment, her dark eyes troubled, as though she still could not grasp the significance of what she was about to say.

"Captain Tremaine handed me a package," she resumed. "It contained two objects that he had fished out of the water alongside the dock from which the *Whiton* had sailed. They were my father's hat and frock coat. His name was printed inside the hatband. Apparently some attempt had been made to burn the hat and coat, but had been given up, and they had been thrown through a porthole into the harbor. They belonged to my father. There was no question about that. And there was no question but what they had been dropped from the *Whiton* before she sailed for California."

Vance Cameron spoke sharply. "What was the date of Tremaine's find?"

"It was on the Monday after the night my father and Ralph Gilmore vanished," Ellen said. "Of course, at that time, Captain Tremaine knew nothing about what had happened in Baltimore. He was puzzled, for it suggested to him that my father had sailed for California. He sailed that same night for Maine, and by the time he arrived in Baltimore, nearly a month later, he had learned of the embezzlement and the disappearances. Because of the respect he held for my father he brought the hat and coat to me instead of going to the authorities.

"The next day a fish-eaten, badly decomposed body was found floating in Chesapeake Bay. It was identified by the clothes that remained as Ralph Gilmore's body. He had been murdered, for the skull had been crushed by a blow. It was Captain Tremaine who brought me that word also and I escaped secretly from my rooming house a few minutes ahead of the officers who came to arrest me.

"I managed to make my way by stagecoach and railroad to Pittsburgh and then to Independence. But my trail had been picked up. The man named Dan Slater who was murdered in Independence was following me, I am sure. I believe he was a detective employed by creditors of the bank, for I know that private agents were watching me during those four weeks in Baltimore."

She quit talking. There was a long silence. It was finally broken by Emery Dixon. "Then this is why you have been so anxious to reach California this season? You hope to intercept this vessel — the *Whiton*?"

"Yes," Ellen said. "I have prayed that it has not been able to make a quick voyage. Otherwise it will be there ahead of me. And if we are snowed in in the mountains . . ." She spread her hands in a hopeless gesture.

"And if you find your father . . . ?" the missionary asked gently.

Tears suddenly streamed down Ellen's face. "Luke has asked me that same question," she choked. "I — I don't know. I don't know!"

Trouble was etched deeply in Emery Dixon's homely face. "I recall more details of the case, now that your story freshens my memory," he said reluctantly. "As I remember, the authorities found a note from you in Ralph Gilmore's room in which you invited him to call for a late supper at your father's home the evening he was mur— he disappeared."

"I did not send that note," Ellen said.

"They said it was in your handwriting," the minister said.

"It must have been sent by someone who imitated my writing."

"Who would do that?" Emery Dixon asked. "And for what purpose?"

"I do not know," Ellen said. Her voice was rising and thinning. The strain had robbed her of all color.

"And you have no witnesses to support your story that you do not know what happened between your father and Ralph Gilmore in the house that night."

With a long, fierce stride Luke moved in, placing his lean height between Ellen and the grim-faced minister. "That's enough," he said hoarsely. "Why torture her? We're not her judge. Nor her jury."

"Torture is not my purpose, I assure you, my son," Emery Dixon said wearily. "I believe Ellen is innocent. Otherwise she would not have revealed her identity to us and placed herself at our mercy. However, we must face facts. All the evidence is that she and her father are guilty. And that is the way a real judge and jury will look at it, I fear."

Luke grasped him by the front of his frayed old coat. "You mean you'd turn her over to the law?"

"That is a question all of us will have to decide in our own consciences when the time comes, Luke," Emery Dixon said.

The old, unbridled wildness and lawlessness raged in Luke. He clutched Emery Dixon tighter, shaking him as he would a rag. But there was no fear in the minister. His gaze met Luke's unwaveringly.

Then the rage subsided in Luke. The emptiness came back — and the futility. His fingers relaxed, releasing Emery Dixon. He turned suddenly and walked out of the camp circle and into the darkness beyond the wagons.

He stood there beneath stars that were tiny and cold through a thin overcast, trying to think clearly — and failing. There was no answer to any of the questions he asked himself. He was in love with Ellen Jessup. He admitted that. But all that the admission brought him was a greater sense of loss and despair.

He finally moved toward the camp again.

And as he neared the wagons he found Cameron standing in the deep shadow of an alder. Remembering Mack Sledge and the ambush back in the Snake River country, he realized that he had been careless again, and that Cameron once more had been his self-appointed protector.

"It's all right," Cameron murmured. "Thorne and Menafee are sitting tight beside their fire, along with their crew."

Luke moved closer to him. "Who are you, Cameron?" he demanded. "What are you? Why are you following her?"

"To arrest her," Cameron said. "For murder. And her father also, if possible."

"I've had the hunch that's the way it was," Luke said.

"I am from the same investigating agency that sent Dan Slater," Cameron said. "In fact my father is head of the agency. We specialize in protecting banks. The Jessup institution was a client. Dan sent word that he had picked up Ellen's trail and needed help. I caught up with them at Independence. Dan was killed the day after I arrived and I, naturally, took over."

"She trusts you," Luke said.

"Yes," Cameron murmured. "She trusts me."

He let it rest there. Presently he went on, "Abbie suspects I am following Ellen. But for mercenary purposes. She evidently believes I am after the stolen money for myself. At first she pitied me as a gambler and a sinner. Now she thinks I am a scoundrel, trying to profit by another person's crime. When she learns the truth — that I am involved in attempting to send to the gallows a girl who looks on me as a friend — she will have still greater reason to despise me."

"I'll stop you if you try to arrest Ellen," Luke said and his voice was without tone.

Cameron said tiredly, "You can't do it, Luke. You've got to see this through with me — to the finish. I know how you feel about Ellen. But this is a matter of murder."

"She's innocent," Luke said stonily. "But her father — he must have written that note to Gilmore. The one that will convict her. He was a banker and clever with a pen, no doubt."

"Perhaps," Cameron said.

"Don't you see?" Luke said, his voice suddenly hoarse. "She has a horror in her. She and her father must have been mighty close. She respected and loved him. All that's keeping her going is the prayer that there must be a big mistake somewhere. She has to find him, hoping that he can explain this thing. If she ever becomes finally convinced that he is guilty, it will be the end of her. It's the way she's made."

"Yes," Cameron said. He turned, gazing into the firelit camp at Abbie. "And Abbie will detest me forever," he added. There was bitter protest in his haggard face as he walked away.

They resumed the march at dawn. Three nights later they camped at the base of the great, rugged mountain wall that barred their path. Beyond those high rims lay California.

It was past midnight when a wild commotion aroused Luke from his blankets. Shouts rose from the darkness. Then he heard the pound of galloping horses, receding westward.

He raced to the point of the disturbance. The Philips brothers had been standing the middle watch over the meager stock herd. A bright moon was in the sky. In its light Luke came upon Bart Philips standing over the sprawled form of his brother, Clint.

"They stole the horses an' killed Clint," Bart Philips mumbled. "Tracy Menafee slugged Clint with his gun when Clint tried to stop 'em. I saw him do it. There was three of 'em."

Cameron arrived. He and Luke bent over Clint Philips. Cameron uttered an exclamation. "He isn't dead!" he said.

Clint Philips had been lucky. He had been struck a glancing blow by the heavy barrel of Menafee's cap-and-ball pistol. By daybreak he was able to talk. "Menafee acted like a wild man," he said. "I ducked or I'd have had a mashed skull."

Al Thorne and Chape Parker were missing with Menafee, along with the only three saddle horses.

"They're making sure they get across the rim before snow comes," Luke told Cameron. "They'll be waitin' for us on the other side or in Hangtown. They know we can't turn back now."

They pushed ahead once more. And now each step was upward.

Chapter XXI

Four days later Luke led the ragged party out of the shelter of timber onto an open mountainside. An icy wind now had its full thrust at them. There was only a handful of them left. The remainder of Menafee's crew had deserted the party on the second day of the ascent and had raced ahead on foot for the pass.

Carrie Philips and two men too ill to walk, rode on blanket pads on the backs of the oxen that were still alive. All other members of the party were on foot, for the last of the wagons had been abandoned during the tortuous climb from Carson Valley.

The first summit of Carson Pass was behind them. It was midmorning now, and they were nearing the second and last summit. They were nearly two miles above sea level. A thin powder of dry snow squealed beneath their worn footgear. This meager blanket of snow was at least a week old and marred only by the passage of Menafee and his men. But the weather that had held off for so long was building up. The belated winter was at hand.

The heatless sun faded slowly into the shroudlike mist that was closing in over the rocky peaks around them. Then it was gone entirely. The pale wind moved through the weather-twisted timber on the ridges. The cold was the blue cold of the high mountains, the cold that thinned the blood and turned a man's resolution to water.

Once over the crest — if they reached it — they would descend to warmer country and find other humans. At the foot of the mountains lay Hangtown. Beyond were Sacramento and the fabled San Francisco. But here was winter and desolation.

And now Luke felt something as cold as a finger of death touch his cheek and rest there. And another.

Snow!

"Faster!" he said. He and Ellen were helping Martha Dixon, lending her their strength. Cameron and Abbie were with Emery Dixon. Only the minister's indomitable will was keeping him on his feet.

The snow came blindingly now, sweeping in a white torrent across the mountain. Luke found Ellen gazing up at him through it. Her dark eyes were big and clear against the thinness of her face. There was an indomitable quality in her also, an invincible spirit. And she was beautiful.

She halted him, brought him around to stand before her. Then she drew his face down to her own and kissed him with a deep tenderness and a wild and longing and abiding passion. Just as abruptly, she drew away, pushing back when he tried to take her in his arms.

"No, Luke," she breathed. "I should not have done that, I know. I could not help it. Forget that I kissed you. Forget everything that concerns me. I — I will not leave you a memory of sorrow."

The wind built up in a fury, hurling the snow savagely at them.

"Faster!" Luke kept saying.

Men stumbled and fell and lay sobbing until he pulled them to their feet and lashed them into motion with his voice. He jeered them and taunted them. They remembered those days back on the Kansas prairie and on the Platte when he had derided them, and they were angered into wanting to live again.

And Emery Dixon, meeting the challenge, tried to sing one of his inspirational songs in a croaking, labored voice. Abbie joined in, then Ellen. And then Luke and Cameron and the others.

"Praise God from Whom all blessings flow,
Praise Him all creatures here below,
Praise Him above, ye heavenly host . . ."

The blizzard raged around them and they defied it. "Hurry!" Luke yelled. "Faster! It can't be much farther. Keep moving. Don't quit now."

They fought onward. They clung to rocks, dragged themselves upward and ahead by will alone.

"Other men made it, and with wagons," Luke kept taunting them. "You have only yourselves. We're almost to the rim. Faster! Faster!"

But he knew the story was almost told. He was now carrying Martha Dixon in his arms. Emery Dixon fell and could not rise. Cameron lifted him over his shoulder.

The snow was deepening around their numbed feet, opposing every step, holding them back. There was no knowing how near or how far was the crest.

Then, for a moment, through a clearing

in the storm, Luke gained a view ahead. At the same time he felt the hostile rise of the earth, relent, and he was staggering ahead — downslope.

"We're over!" he yelled. "Come on, all you brave ones! We're in California! On the right side!"

They stumbled downward, sliding and reeling. Soon the rims around them broke the force of the wind. The snow still fell in a flood, but within a mile they had reached timber that sheltered them. The trail improved.

Just as darkness came they saw a light ahead, thrusting a yellow lance through the falling snow. It came from a window, a cabin window. Other lights appeared, strewn along the bank of the stream they had reached — the American River.

These were the first habitations they had seen since leaving Fort Laramie — and that was a lifetime in the past. They broke into a staggering run and entered this mining camp. Their cries brought bearded men from the warmth of shanties and dugouts to help them.

Amid the confusion Luke glimpsed a familiar figure cross the beam of light that streamed from the door of a cabin. It was Tracy Menafee. He also caught sight of Al

Thorne and Chape Parker. Then they faded off into the background.

He felt Ellen's fingers tighten in fear on his arm. And Cameron murmured. "You were right, Luke. They waited for us."

They were led into a cabin where a tiny stove glowed with its burden of pitch fuel. They gratefully absorbed its warmth. Luke saw that Cameron, as always, was at Abbie's side. But she drew away. Ellen also noticed this while they ate the hot meal the miners set before them. She waited until the four of them were left alone.

Suddenly she said, "You are wrong, Abbie. I am responsible for enough without breaking your heart too — and Vance's. He is not what you suspect. He is watching me, that is true. But not because he is after the money. He is following me to arrest me."

She looked at Cameron. "That is correct, isn't it?"

Cameron was amazed. "How long have you known?" he asked.

"Not until recently," Ellen said. "I began to realize that Luke knew something about you. So I looked back at everything that had happened. And I could see that Dan Slater hardly would have been sent alone on such a task."

"It's true. I have followed Ellen all the way from Independence, expecting that she would lead me to her father. Then I intended to make the arrests. There is no longer any point in delaying. I must arrest Ellen now on a charge of complicity in murder."

"Handcuffs and all, I suppose?" Luke said coldly.

"No," Cameron said. "At least not so long as you do not attempt to see that she escapes from me. I must ask her to give me the same promise."

"To hell with you," Luke said. "I'll give you no promises."

They stood measuring each other, and the wildness rode Luke's eyes. Ellen thrust herself frantically between them. "No!" she choked. "I will not let you and Vance — it would be monstrous for you two to fight with guns. Why, you've been like brothers! Vance, I will make no attempt to get away from you. I will do what you say."

"I must ask you to accompany me to San Francisco in the hope we can find this ship you say is named the *Whiton*," Cameron said reluctantly. "I hope to start as soon as possible. In the morning if it can be arranged."

Ellen nodded. "Very well," she said with an effort.

"I will go with you, Ellen," Abbie said, and took her hand.

Luke sat for a long time, his hands, thinned by toil and privation, lying flat before him on the rough table. Ellen watched him, waiting. She finally said, "No, Luke."

"But I've got to know," he said. "I've got to know what happens to you. I'll go with you."

The four of them arrived at Hangtown in the forenoon of the second day aboard a rude ranch wagon that served as a stage over the rough trails from the mountain camps.

Hangtown was a sea of mud, for what had been snow on the high passes was rain at this lower altitude. From the window of an eating house they presently saw three horsemen splash into town. They watched Tracy Menafee and his companions inquire at the stage station. The trio glanced toward the eating house, then mounted and vanished down a side lane.

"They'll never quit," Cameron said. "If they ever put you and me out of the way, Luke, and get their hands on Ellen . . ."

They returned to the stage station and bought fare on a run that was slated to leave within a few minutes for Sacramento.

Luke buttonholed the stationmaster.

"We're just off the trail from Independence," he said. "And anxious about news of a bark named the *Whiton* that sailed from New York for San Francisco Bay a few months ago. Do you happen to have heard anything about her?"

"Shucks, mister," the man snorted. "There're more ships in Frisco bay than ants in a jampot. Hundreds of 'em. How would I know about this one you mention way up here in Hangtown?"

Luke, shrugging, turned to rejoin Cameron and the girls. But a man touched his arm, halting him. The stranger was a miner by his garb, and had just alighted from a newly arrived stage, along with a dozen other passengers.

"I'm just back from Sacramento, friend," the man said. "I heard what you asked the agent. There's a vessel named the *Whiton* lyin' in the river at Sacramento. They told me she's been there more'n two weeks, waitin' out a quarantine."

Ellen and the others had moved nearer. "The *Whiton*?" Ellen breathed. "At Sacramento?"

"Quarantine?" Luke exclaimed. "Does that mean the passengers are still aboard?"

"I reckon," the man said. "It seems like a couple o' cases o' yellow fever broke out a'ter the *Whiton* had cleared from Panama fer California. They wouldn't let her dock at San Francisco till she had sat out twenty-one days to make sure she was clean o' yellow jack. Bein' as most o' her passengers was bound fer the gold country anyway they decided to move up river to Sacramento. I heerd them say this mornin', as I was waitin' to board the stage, thet her quarantine was up today."

"Today?" Ellen echoed.

Luke saw that she was taut and trembling. Now that the showdown was so near she feared to face it.

Their coach arrived at the loading step at that moment, and the driver began calling the way stations on the route to Sacramento. Luke saw her gaze swing to him. As though she had found her answer, she said in a low voice, "Come. This is our stage."

They were silent throughout the long, jolting afternoon, jammed among miners who were bound for Sacramento or San Francisco with gold dust in their pokes to spend on sprees.

Luke sat next to Ellen, their shoulders pressed against each other. Only once did she touch him otherwise. Then she laid her hand on his for a moment. "To think," she murmured, "that I once imagined that I thoroughly detested you."

Abbie remained straight and rigid alongside Cameron. But Luke noticed that she no longer made a point of shrinking away from the dark-eyed man.

It was nearing twilight when the stage unloaded them at the Sacramento station which stood on a wide, muddy thoroughfare facing the levees.

The river front groaned and strained and roared with the worry of the gold rush. Floating craft of all varieties were tied up along the newly built docks or were anchored in the stream. There were many steamboats. Towering above them were the masts and spars of sailing craft, for the river was navigable this far from tidewater for seagoing vessels of light tonnage.

They picked their way through the mud to firmer footing on the docks. Luke approached a man whose garb indicated that he might be a ship's officer.

"We're looking for a bark-rigged vessel named the *Whiton*, sir," he said. "Could you point her out to us?"

"The *Whiton*?" the man said. "The one they sulphured yesterday for yella jack? Why, that's her that's movin' into berth there off to port, my friend. They give her a clean bill o' health this afternoon."

Luke whirled, peering at a sailing vessel, salt-streaked and weathered from a long voyage, that was being warped alongside a dock nearby, her crews chanting at the capstans as they wore the vessel around.

"May God be merciful!" Abbie breathed.

That was all that was said. They stood waiting. Luke felt the aching agony which he knew held all of them. This was Ellen's final moment of ordeal. After all the striving, all the miles and the hardships and the months of danger and companionship, this was perhaps the end and the parting for them.

At the stage station across the way, another crowded coach that had been only minutes behind their own vehicle during the trip from Hangtown, had now pulled in and was discharging its fares.

Among the arrivals were Tracy Menafee and Thorne and Chape Parker. They at once walked with long, hurried strides to the street and gazed around. Then they singled out Luke and his companions on the levee.

Meanwhile the *Whiton* had been winched alongside the landing. A gangplank was dropped. Down it poured a stampeding stream of passengers, whooping with joy at their escape from the confinement that had maddened them for months.

It seemed to Luke that Ellen stopped living as she stood there scanning every face. It was as though her heartbeat had ceased and all her existence was suspended.

Then she spoke, and her voice was so faint Luke barely could hear. "Ralph! Ralph!"

In the next instant, as though she had grasped life again in all its power, she screamed wildly, clearly, "Ralph! Ralph Gilmore!"

Her outcry cut through the drone of activity on the wharves, reached so far that faces a hundred yards away turned toward them.

A man who had been descending the gangplank among the last of the arrivals halted frozen, his eyes, startled and suddenly desperate, searching the swirl of humanity on the river front.

He was a slender, tall man of about thirty, Luke judged, and his jaws and chin were covered by a soft brown beard. Luke had the impression that the beard was strange to its wearer, as though it had been grown during the sea voyage for purposes of disguise. He wore a seaman's knitted cap and peacoat and these too seemed out of place, for there was about him the indefinable posture and air of a man who had been more accustomed to sitting at a desk.

Ellen gathered her skirts and ran nearer, staring with numbed wonder. "It — it *is* you, Ralph!"

Then she screamed again, pointing at him. "You *are* alive! Why — why — you did it yourself, Ralph! It's my father who is dead! Murdered! And you killed him!"

The slender man dropped the dufflebag he was carrying. He leaped to the levee, shoved bystanders aside and raced down the river front.

Luke, impeded for a moment by spectators and by a passing wagon, pursued the fleeing man. Cameron was at his heels.

"Of course!" Cameron panted. "Of course! How stupid of me! That body in Chesapeake Bay was really Ellen's father on whom Gilmore had planted his own clothes and ring."

Their quarry darted into the open door of a big, gloomy freight shed that fronted on the wharves. Luke and Cameron followed.

They pulled up. The interior was black and unlighted. As their eyes adjusted somewhat, Luke saw that the structure was two hundred feet or more in length and nearly half that in width. It was so newly built that the air was spiced with the tang of resin and fresh-cut pine. Out of the shadows on either hand loomed great mounds of cargo — barrels and bales and casks. At intervals along the walls, bands of gray daylight from the misty outer twilight came through the open wagon ports, big enough to accommodate horse-drawn trucks.

They could hear the pound of Gilmore's footsteps somewhere in the shadows. Then, so faintly they could not exactly define them, came other sounds. Then silence.

"Stay here!" Luke said to Cameron. He raced ahead.

He stopped abruptly. He could hear those other movements more plainly now . . . as though they might be coming from more than one source.

He moved ahead again and was forced to cross one of the islands of light.

Instantly a gun roared from the gloom ahead of him. The bullet passed so close to his head its sound was a deadly snakelike buzz in his eardrums.

His pistol was in his hand, but he held his fire. He did not dare chance killing

Ralph Gilmore. The man must be taken alive.

Crouching, he raced with straining strides toward the point from which the shot had come. The gun exploded again, deafeningly. The flash seemed to leap into his eyes. And a second pistol to his left, but several yards away, also lashed out at him.

There were at least two of them. But both bullets had missed. Then he collided with a figure in the darkness. He slashed out with the muzzle of his pistol, and missed. But the fingers of his left hand caught and held a man's throat.

At the same moment the gun to the left opened up again, firing twice. In the lightning flicker of the powder flame Luke saw the face of the man he had grasped.

It was Chape Parker. Menafee and Thorne and Parker must have flanked the warehouse and entered by way of the ports.

Ralph Gilmore or Henry Jessup — it did not matter to them. One or the other held the secret of the location of the stolen money. Now, they too wanted Ralph Gilmore alive, so that he could talk. But they wanted him for themselves.

All this drove through Luke's mind as he felt Chape Parker sinking in his grasp.

There was a choked, bubbling sound from the man. "You — you've killed me, Al," Parker gasped. Then he sagged to the floor. Al Thorne's bullets had found, not Luke, but his own comrade.

Thorne's gun exploded twice more. Luke fired three times into the powder flashes, thumbing the hammer as fast as his finger could move. He fired once again and this time he heard the hard smash of his slug through flesh, heard a man's convulsive gasp and a body fall.

Now shooting started at the far end of the building. Luke realized that this was Cameron's gun.

Tracy Menafee's voice, high with fear, desperate with the need to ward off death, now began shouting surrender.

Silence followed. Then Cameron said harshly, "Walk into the light where I can see you, Menafee. With your hands up. And if that's Ralph Gilmore with you, let him do the same."

Luke saw two figures emerge from the shadows. Gilmore, in his flight through the warehouse, must have run into the arms of Menafee and his men.

Luke walked cautiously toward the point where he had heard his bullet strike. There he found Al Thorne's body. The slug had torn through his chest. And Chape Parker was dead also.

"Luke!"

It was Ellen's voice, prayerful, pleading, but without hope. She had entered the building even while the shooting was going on. And Abbie too was in the warehouse which was acrid with powder smoke. Luke heard the rush of skirts as she raced to where Cameron stood confronting Menafee.

"Luke!" Ellen called despairingly again.

Then she found him. She touched him timidly at first, then with a wild hope. "Are you — ?" she asked.

"I'm all right," Luke said. "Not a scratch."

He took her in his arms. He kissed her, and then he held her there for a long and fulfilling moment. She clung to him with a desperate strength, saying over and over again, "I'll never let you go! Never!"

Presently they went to help Cameron with his prisoners. Neither Menafee nor Ralph Gilmore had been injured during the fight. Cameron lodged them both in the town lockup and arranged for reliable men to stand guard over them.

In addition to charges of conspiracy against Luke's life that Cameron intended to bring, Menafee was accused of assault with intent to kill in connection with the slugging of Clint Philips. He faced certain indictments and conviction, for, even more heinous in the eyes of the miners, was the fact that he had broken the unwritten law of the trail by deserting his comrades in an attempt to save himself. That, Luke knew, ranked as almost a capital crime in the code of the stampeders who were certain to sit on the juries in the newly organized state.

Ralph Gilmore would await extradition to the East to stand trial for the murder of Ellen's father. Gilmore told the whole story. He had methodically robbed the bank, laying plans to place the blame on Henry Jessup and to take passage to California. He had imitated Ellen's handwriting, and had left the forged note along with the other evidence he had manufactured to make it appear that Henry Jessup and his daughter had connived his own murder.

"You were so damned scornful of me," he flashed at Ellen. "If you'd have married me, none of this would have happened. I wanted to see you dragged in the mud — you and your devilish pride."

Gilmore confessed that he had slain Henry Jessup with a blackjack that night while Ellen slept in her room. He had traded clothes with his victim and donned a false beard and mustache. Then helping himself to the banker's carriage, he had made sure he would be glimpsed driving out of Baltimore at midnight. He had dropped Henry Jessup's body in the bay, then made his way to Philadelphia in another carriage that he had acquired secretly beforehand. From there he had gone by night train to New York to board the *Whiton*.

They found the money in a trunk that Gilmore had shipped on the *Whiton*. Cameron arranged with the Sacramento authorities to have it stored in the only iron safe in Sacramento big enough to contain the stacks of yellowbacks and bags of gold coin.

Wearily Luke and Cameron and Ellen and Abbie walked through the chill, damp darkness and muddy streets of Sacramento town in search of lodging.

They found an inn. Ellen stared at the painted sign over the door. Its name was the Overland Inn. Suddenly she began to sob, and then to laugh hysterically. "The Overland Inn!" she wept. "Where — where I first laid eyes on you, Luke."

Abbie was walking at Cameron's side,

her piquant face wan. Then Cameron suddenly lifted her bodily in his arms so that her feet were far off the ground. He kissed her with all the hunger of a man who has long been refused.

"We're going back to Hangtown tomorrow," he said.

"To Hangtown?" Abbie murmured. "Why, pray tell?"

"Your uncle is a minister," Cameron said. "He marries people, as you well know. Or isn't that reason enough?"

"Reason enough," she sighed. "And high time too."

Luke looked down at Ellen. "Hangtown?" he asked.

All the secrets and all the shadows and all the barriers were gone from her dark eyes. And all the loneliness from his heart. She kissed him with the fullness of a woman's yearning and warmth and tenderness.

"Hangtown first," she said. And her heart was dancing in those dark eyes now, and in her voice. "And then — anywhere. Oregon, Taos, it doesn't matter. I've learned to cook. I can drive oxen. I've skinned antelope and dressed buffalo meat. I'll even try these boudins you talked about."

She paused. "But, one thing," she said

positively. "There will be no more Spanish señoritas, no matter where you go. For I will scratch out their eyes."

The four of them stood laughing in the dim light that streamed from the entrance to the inn. The rain had set in again, but they did not know it. Then they went into Sacramento's Overland Inn arm in arm.